GREYHOUND
THERAPY

GREYHOUND
THERAPY

JR CONWAY

CITI OF BOOKS

CITIOFBOOKS, INC.
3736 Eubank NE Suite A1
Albuquerque, NM 87111-3579
www.citiofbooks.com
Hotline: 1 (877) 389-2759
Fax: 1 (505) 930-7244

Ordering Information:
Quantity Sales. Special discounts are available on quantity purchases by corporations, associations, and others. For details, contact the publisher at the address above.

Printed in the United States of America.

ISBN-13   Paperback   978-1-962366-26-7
               eBook   978-1-962366-27-4

Library of Congress Control Number: 2023917962

TABLE OF CONTENTS

CHAPTER 1

A strong gust of wind struck the unmarked cruiser broadside. Sheriff Craig Spence leaned forward in the passenger seat and peered through the windshield. Clouds were building up in the southwest, and winds were kicking up prairie dust. Steve Lolly, Craig's chief deputy, was driving. He tightened his grip on the steering wheel as another gust broadsided the cruiser and said, "In for some weather, I think."

"Let's check it," Craig said. He changed stations from country Western music to a Rock Springs station that does mostly news and weather.

"With sustaining winds of forty to forty-five miles per hour, capable of bringing up to six inches of snow to the area. Expect blowing snow and icy driving conditions," the announcer was saying.

"So now you're a weatherman?" Craig asked with friendly sarcasm. "That was a good call."

"Boss, for years I've told you that my capabilities are undervalued," Steve quipped.

"Don't push it," Craig responded. "I just may start paying you what you're worth." Craig glanced at the green highway sign announcing they were sixteen miles to Rock Springs.

Winter driving in this part of Wyoming wasn't for the faint of heart. Below zero temperatures and windblown snow combined with black ice conditions and heavy vehicle traffic set the stage for some horrific accidents. Like that time two years ago . . .

Craig and Steve were on this same stretch of road in a blinding snowstorm, traveling ten to fifteen miles an hour. Steve was driving, and the only way he could tell he was on the road was by picking out the reflectors on the snow poles every hundred feet or so just off the right shoulder. Keeping watch for the poles, Craig had noticed flashing emergency lights off the road.

"Pull over, Steve!" Craig had shouted. "Somebody might be hurt." Steve had pulled off the highway as far as he dared and turned on the cruiser's overhead emergency lights, casting a red hue through the blowing snow and surrounding area. Craig made out two figures standing next to a small car, nose down in the drainage ditch. After struggling with the door against the wind, Steve was able to make his way over to the disabled vehicle. That's when things went south.

Through the blowing snow, Steve had seen the headlights swinging erratically right to left. Then there were the running lights of a trailer sliding sideways toward the cruiser. Instinctively, Steve had scrambled up the embankment on the far side of the ditch and watched helplessly as the big rig slid out of control into the left side of the cruiser, launching the car with Craig in it into the ditch and becoming wedged under the rear end of the hapless little car already there

He had been disoriented, and the blowing snow was stinging his face. It took some time for him to realize that the windshield was gone. In the flashing light, he could see the underside of a car. He had tried to move, but the seat had come forward and pinned him against the dash. A strong odor was filling the air around him. He began to panic as he came to recognize what it was.

"Gasoline fumes!" he'd said out loud. "There's a gas leak!" he had yelled out, hoping someone could hear him above the wind.

"Dear God, if I gotta die, please don't let me burn," he had prayed as he continued trying to free himself. "Please, God, no fire," he kept repeating as desperation took hold of him.

"Hey, boss, you okay?" Steve was yelling at him from the back seat.

"Get the seat off me before this thing blows, and be careful—no sparks," Craig recalled pleading.

Steve and the occupants from the other car had used their combined strengths, pulling and tugging on the seat back. Each time they pulled;

Craig got a little more wiggle room. Finally, he had been able to sit up and, using both feet against the floor, pushed as hard as he could. There had been a loud snap, and Craig rolled into the backseat. Fortunately, the rear door on the driver's side had sprung open when the trailer hit. On his hands and knees, he had crawled out into the snow.

Craig chuckled and prodded Steve playfully with his elbow.

"What, boss?" Steve asked.

"I was just remembering that crash we were in and all of us trying to get out of that hole at the same time," Craig said, laughing as he spoke. "Arms and legs everywhere. Wonder we didn't kill one of us."

"We must have been some sight, huh, boss?"

"I thought I was a goner for sure. Thank God, it didn't burn." As he was speaking, Craig noticed that they had entered the city limits.

Rock Springs, Wyoming, was thought of by many as the ugly little town that straddles Interstate 80 about 250 miles West of Cheyenne, Wyoming, and about one hundred miles east of Salt Lake City, Utah. It was established as a mining town in the 1800s, and it was now the largest town in Sweetwater County and had a colorful history.

In 1886, for the very first time anywhere, the national guard was deployed in Rock Springs to quell violence between Eastern European miners and Chinese laborers. Hundreds of Chinese were killed, and the melee became known as the Great Chinese Massacre.

In the early 1970s, Rock Springs was put on the map again when CBS aired a documentary portraying the town as an example of the "Wide Open Wild West," with a municipal government laced with corruption, the epicenter of a prostitution circuit that stretched from Colorado Springs, Colorado, to Salt Lake City, Utah, and open gambling. Craig recalled that the fallout from the exposé had nearly ruined the town. Longtime friends were pitted against one another, and he had to arrest people he'd known all his life. Some went to prison, others were exonerated, but their lives were changed forever.

Steve drove through town, staying on I-80. Craig lived eleven miles west of Rock Springs in the town of Green River, the county seat of Sweetwater County.

"It's been a long day," Craig said as he glanced at the car's dash clock. It was 4:45 PM.

"Yes, sir," Steve replied through a yawn. "I'll just drop you off at the house, and I'll see you in the morning."

"Deal," Craig replied, reaching in the backseat to retrieve his briefcase and jacket.

Craig opened the door and stepped out into a stiff breeze. He glanced at the sky as the car pulled away. Clouds were overhead, and there was the rumbling of thunder off to the south. It was rush hour in Green River, and several passing cars had blown their horns in greeting. Each time, Craig would wave, recognizing no one, just waving so that people wouldn't think their hello had been wasted.

When Craig stepped out on the front stoop the following morning, it was still snowing, and the wind nearly took his hat off. Holding his hat with one hand, he pulled the parka collar tight around his neck. Glancing over his shoulder, he could see his wife, Martha, through the bay window, standing as she did every morning, still in her bathrobe, watching him cross the street safely. He let go of the collar long enough to give her a quick wave, tilted his head against the wind, and stepped out into the street. It was slick, and it took some fancy footwork to keep his balance. *Wearing cowboy boots today is a bad idea,* he thought to himself. Taking short deliberate steps, he made it to the landing atop the courthouse steps without falling. Before opening the front door, he looked back at the bay window. Martha was gone. He made it across the street safely, and she was about whatever would occupy her day.

Physically, Craig Spence would not be considered a large man. He stood about five foot ten and weighed a little less than two hundred pounds. He had been on the navy boxing team during the Korean War, which accounted for his chiseled appearance. He was broad shouldered, and his torso was sculptured to the waist. His arms were well muscled, and his hands were like those of a farmer, thick and powerful looking.

For nearly twenty years, Craig had been sheriff of Sweetwater County. Many of the county's residents had grown into adulthood on his watch. The respect he enjoyed could be attributed to his direct and personal involvement in their development—father figure and mentor to some and the deliverer of a swift kick in the buttocks to others.

The cleaning crew was still milling around when Craig entered the courthouse lobby.

"Good morning, Sheriff," came the greeting from an elderly woman swinging a dry mop over the tiled lobby floor.

"Hi ya, hi ya," responded Craig. That's the way he said hello to everyone. "How's things at home?"

"The kids are all out of the house, so life is good," she said. They both laughed, and Craig continued across the lobby toward his office. It was located in an annex at the back of the courthouse.

"Hey, Craig, how ya doing?" A portly man in his late fifties to early sixties was sort of rolling down the hall toward him.

"Hi ya, hi ya, Fred. Are you okay?" Craig asked as Fred extended his hand. The sheriff didn't shake hands like most folks. He didn't just extend his hand; he thrust it forward all the way from the shoulder as if he were delivering a body blow. As he grasped Fred's hand, he covered the clasped hands with his left and gave a couple of good pumps.

"How's your wife?" Craig asked as they relaxed their hands.

"She still thinks she can beat me up," Fred responded. This brought a big grin to Craig's face as he remembered back ten years ago. He used to pick Fred up at his house every weekend and take him to jail for his own protection. His wife would beat him up and threaten to feed him to the coyotes.

Craig's office was virtually a static history of the Sweetwater County Sheriff's Department. The walls were lined with awards and certificates, pictures of previous sheriffs and of Craig with dignitaries, including governors, senators, congressmen, notable law enforcement icons, and presidential candidates. In a glass display case against one wall was a collection of drug paraphernalia and weapons. The desk was piled high with budget documents, statistical reports, and stuff to be signed. Culling these stacks was the way most mornings were spent. A spindle in the center of the desk had a "while you were out" message stuck to it. Craig read it without taking it off. The message read, "Josh Betinoli, hospital administrator, Memorial Hospital, needs to talk with you ASAP." The desk and executive chair surrounded by chairs were strategically placed to give a sitting room appearance.

Over coffee a week ago, Josh had mentioned that his security people were being overwhelmed due to an influx of persons being held in emergency detention. He'd like some relief from the sheriff's office. What Josh really wanted was for the SO to take responsibility for the security in the detention unit like state statute dictates. According to Wyoming Statute, a person who was considered a danger to him or herself—or to others—could be detained against their will for seventy-two hours during which time their status would be evaluated by a physician and the county court. A hearing was generally held prior to the seventy-two hours expiring at which a determination would be made to release the detained person or hold for further treatment or evaluation. The person could then be held an additional seven days. Throughout this period of detention, security personnel must be present 24/7 to protect the detained, the hospital staff, and the patients. The statute also stated that the safety of the person in detention was the responsibility of the county sheriff.

Craig had discussed the matter with his staff and had been assured that there would be overtime and manpower issues that would complicate compliance. There was no provision in the department budget to place a deputy at the hospital 24/7, run a jail, and maintain an effective patrol operation and an investigative division. Craig knew he had to find a solution, and he needed some answers before he met with Josh.

The first of Craig's staff to show up for the daily briefing was Sherrie Munson, his jail administrator. Sherrie, a woman of considerable girth, could have graced the backfield of any football team. Her broad shoulders complemented her hips that were supported by short sturdy legs that jutted out the bottom of her tan uniform skirt. Her shirt, neatly pressed with captain's bars on the collars, was barely managing to restrain her bosom. Her dark hair neatly cropped around her head gave her face a matronly appearance.

Sherrie was the widow of a former deputy that had worked for the sheriff that Craig defeated for the job. The deputy had been one of the few Sweetwater law enforcement officers that had lost their lives in the line of duty. He had been ambushed while checking out a complaint about a house being used for prostitution.

Sherrie had two teenaged sons that were still in high school, and without their dad around were giving her a tough time. When Craig became sheriff, he stepped in and provided some guidance for the boys. With the help of the high school football coach, they were kept headed in the right direction.

Before Sherrie had begun to raise a family, she had worked a few years as a shift commander at the state penitentiary. Supporting those boys was not easy on the meager survivor's pension she got from the state. To make matters worse, there was a good probability that she was going to lose her house. The bank that held the mortgage had already sent her two letters threatening foreclosure. Since he had campaigned on bringing some experience to the department, Craig brought Sherrie on as his jail administrator.

"Morning, Sheriff." Her voice was almost a sigh.

"Hi ya, Sherrie. You gettin' enough rest?" Craig asked, genuinely concerned.

"Last night was not a good night," she began. "The PD brought in two guys they took off the ten-thirty bus for assaulting an old man. They've been a real pain in the ass. Didn't get out of here till two o'clock this morning."

"What's their problem?" Craig asked.

"They're both nuts. Threatening to kill each other. Couldn't split 'em up 'cause it's a full house back there. Every time we'd leave 'em for a minute, the fight was on . . ."

Calvin Watson and Albert Brown had met in a homeless shelter in Barstow, California. They engaged in thefts and burglary to support the unsavory lifestyle they enjoyed. The Barstow police had cut their escapades short when Watson set off a silent alarm in a local gun shop they were burglarizing. The two of them spent several days in the

Barstow City Jail until Brown convinced his elderly mom, who lived in Sacramento, to send $1,500 to a Bondsman so the two of them could be free until trial.

Once out of jail, Brown decided that they should work the streets in the nightlife section of town until they could muster enough money for a bus ticket out of there. Watson didn't really want to do that, but he didn't want to make Albert mad. He had seen him hurt people. He also had no desire to stick around for trial, so he moved in and out of bars and nightspots on one side of the streets while Albert took the others, hitting up customers for change and dollar bills under the pretext of needing a meal.

On the second night, Brown had gotten lucky. He entered a nightspot called the Odyssey and approached a male patron in one of the booths. The man was well dressed, probably a salesman of some kind that had exceeded his limit. He was having difficulty holding his head upright and was nodding and never opening his eyes. On the table was a fifty-dollar bill, two twenties, and several other bills. Taking advantage of the dim lighting and the inattentiveness of people in adjacent booths, Brown scooped up the bills and eased his way back onto the street. Meeting up with Watson, they decided to buy a Greyhound bus ticket and ride as far as the money would take them. Stealing and begging and using the Greyhound, Brown and Watson leapfrogged across the country till they reached Rock Springs, Wyoming.

Steve Lolly and Detective Kevin Marcy entered the room. They reminded Craig of Mutt and Jeff, the old cartoon characters. Steve was small in stature, standing 5'8" and couldn't have weighed more than 135 pounds. His tan uniform was impeccable, form fitting, and the office lights reflected off his highly polished brass.

Steve was one of the first deputies Craig hired when he became sheriff. His wife had just died of cancer, and he was trying to raise two little girls on a stocker's salary at City Market, the local grocery store. Craig had known Steve since before he graduated from high school. Steve's dad had died in a hunting accident, and Craig looked after the family until Steve's mom moved after he got out of school and shortly thereafter he married. Craig had become so much a part of Steve's life that he had been asked to be the oldest daughter's godfather.

When Craig had asked Steve to be one of his deputies, there was some reluctance to accept. He had never contemplated being a deputy. He'd seen what the local cops and deputies got involved in and wasn't sure he was cut out for it, but Craig finally convinced him that there was much more to it than breaking up fights and keeping wives from whipping their husbands or vice versa.

Kevin, 6'4" and a good 240 pounds, also looked like he stepped from the pages of a magazine advertising police uniforms. He'd been an athlete in college and still kept himself in good shape. He kept his hair cut military style and wore a neatly trimmed mustache.

Kevin had lobbied Craig for a job during the days before the election. No matter where Craig was campaigning, walking the streets or holding meetings, Kevin was always there when he wasn't on duty with the Rock Springs Police Department. He did have a good track record as a detective, and Craig had always admired his doggedness when he worked a case. He also had a reputation of being a lady's man, and rumor had it that he was overly friendly with some of his fellow officer's wives. After convincing Craig that he wanted to put all that behind him, he was brought on as investigative division chief.

Craig checked his watch. It was 7:27 AM, and everyone was present for the seven-thirty meeting. After greetings all around, Craig got down to business.

"Steve," he said, "I need you to come up with a plan to handle the hospital situation."

"Boss, I've got a temporary plan, but you're not going to like it," Steve said.

"Try me."

Steve took a sheet of paper off a clipboard he was carrying and walked it over to Craig's desk. He placed it in front of him and had used a finger to guide Craig through the lines and numbers.

"I've got nine patrol deputies that work the metropolitan area. Three shifts, three men each." Steve had paused and looked at Craig, trying to get an indication that he was with him so far.

"Go on," Craig had encouraged.

"I can designate one deputy on each shift each day to be prepared to respond to a hospital call," Steve continued and was interrupted by Craig.

"You're right. I don't like it," said Craig. "What if the deputy is on a call, an accident, or something else happens?"

"The three of us," Steve went on, "Sherrie, Kevin, and me—we're on call. When a call comes in, the one that's on call goes immediately to the hospital, gets an understanding of the situation, relieves the hospital guard, and stands by until the deputy gets there."

"Those calls come in at all hours of the day and night!" Kevin exclaimed. "Two or three in the morning, ten o'clock at night, generally whenever a bus comes in. Surely you're not serious."

"Got a better plan?" Steve asked.

"You said this plan is temporary," Craig butted in. "What's plan B?"

"When we have a crime scene that needs protecting, we call that security company that's run by two ex-cops," Steve reminded everyone. "We've had good luck with them, and they've got sharp people working for them," he continued. "If the price is right, why not hire them to do this?"

The coming of the oil and gas industries to the county in 1980 increased the transit population three times, which was already there, working the coal and trona mines. Housing was not available, and people were camped anyplace that had a bare spot. Tents, campers, cars and trucks, buses and motor homes dotted the landscape on all sides of town and along the highways leading into town. Crimes of all sorts forced the sheriff's patrol division to place its deputies on twelve-hour shifts. Domestic violence, theft, and burglary kept the metro patrol meeting themselves coming and going. The deputies in the outlying areas of the county were bogged down with equipment thefts of hundreds of oil rigs, pumping stations, and maintenance shacks. Coupled with the frequent unidentified human bodies that kept cropping up throughout the county, the department was manpower poor and ineffective.

The major oil companies in the area sought relief by hiring the local security company, Corporate Protection, Inc., popularly known as CPI, to protect their installations and rolling stock. There was a reduction in the number of thefts being reported, but the department still couldn't muster the manpower to protect the crime scenes and conduct proper investigations.

It was Kevin Marcy, the chief of the investigative division, who came up with the idea. The thought was that if the department's manpower could be augmented by security officers, crime scenes could be protected, and the deputies could move on to something else. These people on the scene would also allow the evidence to be preserved and prevent contamination until investigators could get in the area and properly process it.

"The cost of overtime alone would justify giving it a try," Kevin had lobbied. "It would also improve our response capability in the outlying areas of the county," he had suggested.

CPI was owned and operated by a husband-and-wife team, Fred and Amy Dreskel, both former police officers, out of Colorado. They had a good reputation in the community. The company had grown from providing security at special events and hotel bars to securing government facilities in seven states. Their people were well trained and conducted themselves professionally.

After analyzing the pros and cons, Craig had decided to give it a try. An arrangement was made with CPI, and the owners were made special deputies, allowing them under most circumstances to act on behalf of the department. The arrangement worked so well that over time, CPI people were used to transport prisoners, personal protection for visiting dignitaries, and the serving of court documents.

There had been a lull in the conversation as Craig mulled over Steve's plans.

"Sheriff, these people have saved me hundreds of man-hours," Sherrie spoke up. "I've even used 'em to help out in court."

"I agree. They've been great, but why don't we use the hospital situation as a basis to bring on more deputies?" Kevin asked.

"Ain't gonna happen, not this year and maybe not the next," Craig announced. "Steve, you meet with CPI. See if they can take this on and how long it would take them to gear up. I'll meet with Josh and see what he's looking at." He shifted his attention to Sherrie.

"Sherrie, anything special?" he asked.

"Seven going to court this morning. All will probably get bond and free up some beds," she responded. "Those two nuts back there will be arraigned too. They're going to be trouble. Both are wanted in California."

"What's their problem with each other?" Craig asked.

"The real crazy, last name Brown, claims the other, last name Watson, ratted him out to the cops last night about a wallet that was stolen on the bus. Right now, Brown is cuffed to the bars so he can't get to Watson. Soon as I get some room, I'll split 'em up."

"What's on your plate, Kevin?" Craig continued canvassing his staff.

"Located some drilling equipment stolen out of the oil patch," Kevin replied. "It showed up in Utah. I'm meeting with Utah Troopers this afternoon . . ."

If Kevin intended to say anything more, he didn't get the chance. A deputy from the jail had burst into the room, gone straight to Sherrie, and whispered in her ear. The color had slowly drained from her face as she got to her feet.

"What's up?" Craig asked.

"Brown slipped the cuffs," she said. There was a slight pause and she continued, "They think Watson's dead."

CHAPTER 2

The rest of Craig's day was a flurry of activity, though in some ways he was just a bystander. Deputies and police officers flittered around, doing what had to be done while he observed.

Investigating this incident with his people was not a good thing, so following protocol, he called in the Green River Police Department to investigate the death of Calvin Watson. They called in the county coroner who showed up to confirm that Watson was dead and to remove the body to the morgue. As he watched the body being loaded into a van, Craig couldn't help noticing the convenience of the situation. The van, solid black, with Peterson's Mortuary written in large silver letters on the back and each side cargo door, belonged to Glen Peterson, who owned the mortuary and was the county corner. *Glen Peterson had been the county coroner longer than I've been sheriff,* Craig thought.

He made arrangements with the Rock Springs Police Department to temporarily house Albert Brown while the investigation was being conducted and until he could be arraigned. The Rock Springs Police Department had the only padded holding cell in the county. Under the circumstance, Craig wanted to minimize the possibility that the perpetrator would try and do harm to himself.

The cell was one of three holding cells at the PD and was located in the PD's booking area. The front was constructed of bars covered on the outside with heavy-gauged, clear Plexiglas so a prisoner could be watched continuously. The inner three walls were covered with a seamless dark-green padding providing a background which was easy for an observer to detect movement. To make things even better, Brown was dressed in an orange jumpsuit. The only flaw was that the urinal and toilet were in a holding cell next to the padded one.

Satisfied that he had done what he should, Craig didn't want his presence to impede progress. He believed strongly that when you can no longer contribute to the operations at hand, back off, go away, and let people do that for which they were hired.

As he was making his way back to his office, he stopped behind the desk in the booking area—a caged room with an automatic locking door to gain entrance from the outside and an automatic locking door on each end, one leading to the courthouse hallway to the jail administrator's office and the sheriff's office. The other gave access to the bowels of despair, the cell block.

In the room's center wall, about shoulder high for the average person, was a ten-inch-by-three-foot cutout in the mesh and a deputy sitting at a desk. Behind the desk was the space used by Sherrie as her office. That was where Craig spent most of the day coordinating things.

"I'm going to get out of everybody's hair," he said to the deputy on duty. "If anyone needs me, I'll be in my car on my way to Memorial Hospital."

"Yes, sir," the deputy responded.

"Oh! And call Josh Betinoli for me, would ya. Tell him I'm on my way."

It had stopped snowing when Craig stepped out of the courthouse, but the wind was still causing ground blizzards, and the street looked as if it had been polished.

his neck, Craig picked his way to his car. When not in use, the car, an unmarked Ford LTD, was always parked in the same spot where the sign read, "Sheriff—Don't even think about parking here."

He eased his way through town, intent on taking I-80 East back to Rock Springs. Just as he reached the on-ramp, he noticed two county snowplows blocking the eastbound lanes.

Pulling alongside the truck nearest him, Craig recognized the driver as a longtime county employee and road supervisor, Ted Hicks. Craig got out of the car and pulled himself up on the running board of the big truck as the driver rolled down the driver's side window.

"Hi ya, hi ya, Ted, ya old geezer. How ya been?" Craig enthusiastically greeted the truck driver.

"Hey, top cop," he responded through a big toothless smile. "When it snows, all kinds of critters come out, huh?"

"You said it, I didn't. What other than this weather brought you out here?" Craig inquired.

"Over the knoll up ahead, a tractor trailer's being towed off the road," Ted replied. "Highway patrol asked us to block for them."

I-80 out of Green River was a gradual climb to the top of a hill with descending turns on the far side. There was no activity visible from where the roadblock was. "What's keeping you busy these days?" Ted asked. He had to yell down with his head partially out the window because Craig had stepped off the side board and had started back to his car.

"You still read the morning paper?" Craig called out, walking slowly backward.

"Only to check the obituaries!" Ted yelled.

"Be sure and get one this morning!" Craig shouted as he got back in the car.

He reached for the mic hanging on the side of the radio mounted on the center console.

"Dispatch, SO1." A short pause and the radio came alive.

"SO1, Dispatch," a female voice shot back.

"Dispatch, get a call to the hospital administrator. Tell him I'm stuck at a roadblock"

"10-4, SO1." The radio fell silent again.

It was another fifteen to twenty minutes before the tractor trailer crested the knoll being towed by a large tow truck with its blue lights flashing in a staccato-like rhythm with the red lights of the highway patrol car that was bringing up the rear. As they grew closer, the lights on the two snowplows joined in, and Craig smiled at the display.

Ted had backed his plow, clearing a path for traffic to enter the highway. Craig pulled through first and carefully guided the car along the portion of the road that still had snow covering most of the ice. The car held the road well as he slowly increased its speed to thirty-five miles per hour. At this rate of speed, it would take him thirty minutes or so to get to the hospital. He checked the dash clock—it was three thirty in the afternoon already—not much day left, and it would no doubt be a long night.

Sweetwater County Memorial Hospital shared a plateau with Western Community College. On top of College Hill, a causeway connected the main east-west thoroughfare through town, with the north-south thoroughfare in the northern part of the city. The hospital building was a three-tiered structure with the main entrance and access to the emergency room off the parking lot at the second level. The décor blended with the surrounding terrain of sand-colored rocks and high-desert landscaping. Large square windows lined the outside walls of the upper levels, one under the other and one after the other, perfectly distanced apart. Each patient room had a large window.

Craig parked his car and entered the building through the emergency room entrance. There were a few people waiting, but the area was fairly quiet except for the elevator music being piped in.

None of the people waiting nor the person at the registration desk paid any attention as he crossed through the waiting area into the main hallway leading into the interior of the hospital and the administrative offices. Craig made a mental note.

The hospital administrator's office was impressive. Craig walked into a reception area and could see a large conference room and the entrance to a third office. There were pictures of Western scenes on the walls trimmed with mahogany. The waiting room was set up like a living room rather than just a place to wait. The receptionist stood and spoke first.

"You're Sheriff Spence, aren't you?" she asked as she came around the desk to greet Craig. She was very handsome, regal in the way she carried herself, and had a very nice smile. She reached out her hand, and Craig shot out his to grasp it.

"Hi ya, doll," he returned her greeting. "Yes, I'm Craig Spence, and what was your name?" He released her hand and removed his hat.

"I'm Mildred, Mr. Betinoli's secretary," she explained. "Please have a seat. He's been expecting you and will be with you shortly. Can I get you anything, coffee, soda, water?"

"No. No, Mildred, I'm fine."

Craig made his way to a comfortable-looking padded armchair. He had settled in and leaned against the backrest, right into the path of a brightness that blinded. Shifting his body and head, he realized the sun coming through the room's large window caused the brightness, and it reflected off the fish tank in the corner to his right. Red, yellow, silver, and gold flashes emitted from the tank as the fish swam back and forth through the penetrating sunlight.

"Well, Craig, I'm glad you were able to stop by." Josh entered the waiting room and walked toward Craig. His voice was raspy and his face mottled. There was a close resemblance to Colonel Sanders, the fried chicken mogul. His white hair glistened under the office lights, and his white facial hair stood out against the flushed background. Craig lifted himself from the chair and reached out his hand.

"Hi ya, Josh. Wish my shop was as quiet as yours."

"Heard about the excitement at your place this morning," Josh said as they walked to his office. "Surprised you were able to get away."

"After making sure that the scene and the suspect was secure, calling in the other agencies, and setting the investigation in motion, life goes on," Craig explained as he was motioned to sit at a small meeting table in front of Josh's desk. "Anyway, I'm going to be busy enough when the ACLU gets wind of it." Josh settled in at the table with him.

"The ACLU?"

"They filed suit against the county and me—perhaps a year or so back, I think—claiming overcrowding and inhumane conditions."

"So this just adds fuel to the fire, huh?"

"Not only that," Craig started, "these unemployable attorneys don't understand that change takes time. There's studies and bond issues, remodel or new construction site issues, and not-in-my-backyard issues, and I could go on and on, and I'm sure you don't have time to listen, and anyway, we have other things to talk about."

Craig placed his hat on the table in front of him, leaned forward, and looked Josh straight in the eye.

"Josh, ole buddy," he began, "I'm hearing that your security staff is being overwhelmed. Give me an idea of what's happening."

There was a slight pause, and Josh leaned forward on his elbows, his forearms extended, flattening his hands on the table. Craig noticed that Josh's fingernails had been gnawed well back beyond the edges of his fingers.

"Craig, I have a security staff of 8 people to protect a hospital staff of 250 most days, a building consisting of 3 floors with 48 patient rooms, laboratories, testing facilities, operating rooms, emergency room, and a physical plant, including the hospital proper that's located on 40 acres." Josh paused to let what he said sink in. "I run three shifts, two officers per shift, 6:00 AM to 2:00 PM, 2:00 PM to 10:00 PM, and 10:00 PM to 6:00 AM. Most of their time consists of routine security tasks—opening doors, locking doors, checking doors, ensuring unauthorized persons are not where they shouldn't be, assisting staff with the relocation of patients, monitoring the performance of equipment in the power plant, monitoring heating, cooling, and pumping equipment. Then there is the emergency room. Lots of time is spent in this area involving crowd control, dealing with agitated persons, aiding the staff with unruly or violent individuals, and aiding law enforcement officers when they bring people in off the streets and highways."

Craig listened intently and with empathically. Certainly, he could understand operating with not enough manpower.

"Where do you need help?" he asked.

"We're being inundated with admissions that have to be held against their will. We find that many are people who've moved into the area have already been prescribed stabilizing medications, but they've either run out or just stopped taking them. They suffer an imbalance, their behavior or conduct concerns others, they call the police, and the person is determined to be a danger to themselves or others and ends up here."

Josh cleared his throat and walked behind his desk where he had a small cooling unit in which he kept water and other bottled drinks, some alcoholic.

"Want a cool drink, Craig?" he asked.

"Thanks," Craig responded. "Doesn't matter what it is as long as it's wet." Josh sat a bottle of water in front of Craig and took his seat.

"About twice a week, Greyhound buses going east or west puts some one off in Rock Springs because of bizarre behavior," he continued. "I really believe that in restrooms along the way, someone has written: Act crazy on the way to Rock Springs and get a bath, a warm meal, a place to stay and good drugs." They both laughed at this and sipped their drinks, and Josh went on.

"These people from the bus station require special consideration because there's no one to release them to. Most of them are in pretty bad shape mentally by the time they get here. We detain them and have to provide security 24/7. Their first length of stay is seventy-two hours. After a mandatory hearing, the detention could be extended for another seven days, or they could be remanded to the state hospital in Evanston or some other facility. We have to arrange for transport. We're not staffed or equipped for that type of operation. It's really the purview of the sheriff's office by statute."

Craig knew that eventually Josh was going to end up where he did. He stood up, walked over to Josh's desk, and sat on the edge. Josh swiveled in his chair so that he faced Craig when he began to speak.

"Josh, the sheriff's office is in no better shape than you are. We don't have enough people to service this county. We recognize that you're hurting, and we've got a plan, but you have to buy into it." Craig walked back to the table and sat down.

"There's a security company in town that the sheriff's office has been using to augment our staff. We've been satisfied with their work, and they're dependable. We call 'em and they show up. The owners have law enforcement experience, and their people are well trained." He stopped to take a sip of his water and check the expression on Josh's face. It seemed to be a little more flushed than before.

"How would this be put together, and who would they work for?" Josh asked.

"Since I'm the one responsible for the security of those detained, they'd work for me using the same procedures that are used at the jail and following the same policies. We'd have to sit down and come up with a plan to ensure that we operate cooperatively with your staff. No turf disputes, you understand?" Craig again checked Josh's face, and this time, he saw some concern. "Spit it out, Josh," he said.

"I'm in the business of patient care, not running a jail," Josh said.

"True, that's why we'll use my procedures in handling the security aspects, and you can take care of their critter comforts."

"There will probably be conflict between the guards and the nursing staff on the floor."

"Not if they leave security matters to the security officers and follow their instructions. The security people won't get involved with or interfere with medical treatment other than to help your staff when asked. Informing them of how things will work is your job, Josh."

"What about my security staff? Who has the last word on matters pertaining to hospital security?"

"For crying out loud, Josh, let's decide if we want to do this, then we can get the security people together along with our operations people and work out . . ." Craig felt himself getting irritated and decided to go slow.

"Craig, it's an option, but is it the only one we have?" Josh asked.

"From my perspective, it's the only one we have. I'm not able to bring on any more deputies, but I can make some budget adjustments to give me enough dollars to contract with the security company."

"When do you want to start putting it together?" Josh asked.

"Within the next couple of days, I'll have Steve Lolly, my chief deputy, get with you and your security chief and hammer things out. It's a good plan, Josh. It'll be okay." Craig stood up. "I need to get going. After you've had a chance to think on it, give me a call." He picked up his hat from the table and put an arm around Josh's shoulder. They walked together past the receptionist to the door leading back into the hallway.

"Thanks for coming, Craig," Josh said as he shook Craig's hand. "I'll probably be in touch sometime tomorrow. Be careful going home."

"I'll just do that." Craig put his hat on and stepped out into the hall. He passed through the emergency room waiting area, and again, no one looked his way. The big sliding entryway doors opened, and Craig walked out into the parking lot. The winds had died down, but the temperature had fallen. The condition of the streets was somewhat better. Sand trucks had been through, and there was more traction than before. As he entered the highway heading for Green River, it was heartening to see the traffic traveling at forty-five and fifty miles per hour. There were still some icy spots that could ruin your whole day.

Craig got back to the office around five thirty, and copies of reports from his staff about the death of Calvin Watson as well as preliminary reports from the investigative team had been put on his desk. There were also a stack of messages from the local media and one from the chairman of the county commissioners. He wondered how the staff managed to keep all these people at bay.

He began with the reports from his staff and made himself a written summary of events. When he faced the media, he wanted to have a good handle on the situation. When he talked to the county commissioner he wanted to be sure he knew more than the commissioner did. He picked up the report on top of the pile.

"At approximately 7:45 AM, February 8, 1983, Deputy Claude Malinowski was making his security rounds of the adult male section of cells. His first check was cell number 1, which was the drunk tank, in which inmates Albert Brown and Calvin Watson were being housed. Brown was handcuffed to the cell bars, and Watson appeared to be asleep on a mattress on the floor. All of the other cells, number 2 through number 9, had four occupants each, and they were quiet. After checking the female section, Malinowski returned to cell number 1 at approximately 8:05 AM and saw inmate Brown, out of his cuffs, standing and holding inmate Watson's limp body in a choke hold. Utilizing the whistle on his uniform, Deputy Malinowski sounded the alarm, three short blasts on the whistle, and entered the cell. Utilizing his baton, Malinowski forced Brown to release Watson and forced Brown to his knees near the back of the cell."

Craig tried to visualize the scene. Malinowski was 5'11" and weighed around 280 pounds and very little was fat. Brown, on the other hand, was 6'2" tall but wouldn't weigh more than 160 if he were soaking wet. With the help of the baton, Malinowski had no problem enforcing his will. Craig continued reading.

"Deputy Maggie Harris, having responded to the alarm, checked for Watsons vital signs. Finding none, she punched in the 911 code on her handheld radio at 8:10 AM and proceeded to administer CPR. Brown was removed from the cell by Deputy Malinowski and placed in transport restraints, hands secured to a leather belt around his waist and leg irons around his ankles. He was then placed in a sitting position and secured to the cell bars while efforts were made to revive Watson.

"Dr. Cyrus Tate, medical doctor on contract with the county to run the jail dispensary and provide medical services, arrived along with the paramedics at approximately 8:17 AM, and after continued efforts to revive Watson, the doctor pronounced him dead at 8:30 AM.

"The preliminary report from the Green River police verified that death had been caused by strangulation and that Albert Brown was suspected of having deliberately and with intent caused the death of Calvin Watson, and the investigation was ongoing."

Craig picked up the message from the commissioner and dialed his number, and the phone had been answered on the first ring. Craig heard the deep baritone voice of Raul Sosa through the receiver.

"Sosa here. This you, Craig?" Raul asked.

"Hi ya, Raul," Craig replied. "Been looking for me?"

"Where the hell have you been?" Raul asked. "The newspapers and the radio and TV stations have been driving me nuts, and your people—"

"Hey! Hey! Hey!" Craig cut in. "Who put a scorpion in your jockey shorts? All you had to tell them was that the sheriff will make a statement when he has all the facts. Now calm down."

"You have the facts?" Raul asked.

"Sure I do, and I'm about to call the media and make a statement," Craig replied.

CHAPTER 3

"INMATE STRANGLES CELL MATE IN COUNTY JAIL" was the headline splashed across the front of the morning newspaper. The accompanying article took up much of the front page with quotes from county officials, including the sheriff and county attorney's office, the ACLU, the Green River and Rock Springs chiefs of police.

The sheriff had merely confirmed that an incident had occurred in the jail that resulted in the demise of an inmate and that the Green River Police Department was conducting an investigation. He referred all future questions to the investigating agency and the county attorney's office.

The Green River Police Department acknowledged that an investigation of a death at the county jail was in progress and that the case was expected to be turned over to the county attorney soon.

The Rock Springs Police Department affirmed that an inmate that was allegedly responsible for the death of a cell mate at the county jail was being temporarily held at the PD's holding facility, and it was expected that the individual would be transferred back to the county facility as soon as possible and be there for arraignment in county court. No names were released.

Being aware of the legal maneuverings that the county had been involved in over the past year or so, the reporter didn't pass up the opportunity to get comments from the ACLU. The article quoted the ACLU representative as saying that they were planning to file for an injunction against the sheriff, county commissioners, and county attorney, preventing them from holding people in the county jail until pending litigation brought by the ACLU had been addressed by the courts.

Steve and Sherrie read the article as they sipped their morning coffee.

"The ACLU is going to play this for all its worth," she commented.

"Have you ever thought that the ACLU might be the best thing that's happened to us?" Steve looked up from his paper.

Sherrie looked over the top of the paper she was reading with a confused expression on her face.

"These guys are trying to put us out of business, and that's a good thing."

"Sherrie, how long has the sheriff been fighting with the commissioners for a new office building and jail?" Steve paused and then continued. "They've completely ignored any requests he's made. Now he doesn't have to butt his head against the wall. The ACLU can be the bad guys."

"What are the chances they'll be able to get an injunction?" she asked.

"This is just me talking, okay?" Steve cleared his throat before going on. "I look at it this way. There's no other holding facility in this county. Evanston is the closest out of county, eighty miles west. The next closest is Rawlins, where the state penitentiary is, three hours travel time to the east. There's bound to be some movement toward another facility, but I doubt any judge will issue an injunction." He paused. "I've got an appointment with the owner of the security company," he said as he made his way through the booking area. "I need to get this done before the weekend. I'll be on the radio."

Corporate Protection, Inc. operated out of a doublewide mobile home that had been converted to offices and located just off I-80's east frontage road west of Rock Springs. During the middle of the day, there were several white patrol cars and pickup trucks always parked in front. Because temperatures were consistently below zero, each vehicle had an extension cord running from under the hood to an electrical box next to the office entrance. Each patrol unit had a heat lamp in the engine compartment whenever not in use. Security crews working the mines, oil patch, and merchant patrols picked up the vehicles at the beginning of their shifts, and the crews being relived brought them back and plugged them in so the engines would be warm and easy to start when the next shift came on.

Years of law enforcement experience had made Fred and Amy Dreskel recognize the need for a quality security firm in Sweetwater County. Fred had come to Rock Springs in early 1981 to help form a security force at the Sweetwater Power Plant, thirty-five miles east of town. Amy came later that same year and tried to get on the guard force at the plant. Fred had an opening for a security guard, but her resume read like that of someone applying for a chief of police position. He knew that if he hired her, the most he could hope for would be ninety days, and she'd be scooped up by one of the police departments or the sheriff's office. He had visited with her for some time during the interview but finally told her she was overqualified and sent her on her way. He didn't know it, but he'd hear about that assessment long into the future.

Fred tried for several months to convince the company he worked for to expand and take advantage of the opportunities throughout the area. He was finally told, in no uncertain terms, to take care of the plant, forget expanding, or turn in his badge.

In the meantime, Amy secured the director of security position at the mine that supplied coal to the power plant. The power plant was owned and operated by Sweetwater Power and Light, a West Coast corporation, while the coal mine was operated by a subsidiary known as the Sweetwater Coal Company. The only thing separating the mine property and the power plant was a chain-link fence. Sharing common boundaries and having security concerns that were common to both the mine and power plant, Fred and Amy spent much time-sharing information, conducting joint investigations, and getting to know each other.

The entrepreneurial spirit that continued to build inside Fred was so strong that his efforts to suppress it were making his life miserable, and it was becoming obvious that the company no longer had confidence in him. They had begun to keep him at arm's length regarding plans for the company's future or his future with it. He turned in his resignation and decided to start his own security company.

In less than ninety days, Fred had brought on three of his previous coworkers and had negotiated several small contracts with hotels, bars, fast-food restaurants, and car dealerships. The business was beginning to take shape, and he needed someone to help him manage the growth that he envisioned. He called Amy. He never forgot her reaction.

"When I came to you, I just wanted a job," she had begun. "Just wanted to be a security guard with no responsibilities other than doing a security guard's job, but no, I was overqualified. Now you need me. I'm not overqualified now, huh? You son of a bitch! Now you want me to quit the job I finally found for myself and cast my lot with you and your cockamamie idea."

"Was that a yes?" he asked.

"Hell no, we need to talk about this."

Fred and Amy began to have dinner dates. They found that they both enjoyed dancing, so they spent several evenings a week dancing to live music at local lounges that catered to couples their age. They also liked to have a drink, and they were comfortable with each other. They became regulars at nightspots where lawyers, cops, and businesspeople went to unwind. Eventually, the party was not over for Fred and Amy when the music stopped but would continue at Fred's apartment until the wee hours of the morning. It was on one of these occasions when they were fixing breakfast that Fred announced he was moving from his one-bedroom apartment to another apartment building where he would have two bedrooms and could use one for an office.

"What will you do for office furniture?" Amy had asked.

"I suppose I'll be able to find some used fur—"

"I've got a desk, some chairs, and a typewriter," Amy had interrupted.

"You mean you'd give that stuff to me?"

"Not on your life. It's an investment. My contribution to our partnership."

"You're coming aboard!" Fred shouted excitedly.

"Not immediately," she replied. "The contract renewal is coming up at the mine. I think I can arrange for us to get an invitation to bid on it. If we get it, I'm on board."

The relationship between Fred and Amy grew to the point that the entire community expected them to get married. One day without warning, Fred phoned Amy and said, "At four o'clock this afternoon, I'll be in Judge Rucker's Chambers. If you want to get married, be there."

At four that afternoon, Fred Dreskel and Amy Freiberg became Mr. and Mrs. Dreskel.

The very first major contract the two negotiated was to provide security for three years at the Sweetwater Mine. The rest was history. Hotels and bars to corporate protective services to securing government installations . . .

Steve pulled up to the CPI office and flipped on his overheads. The pulsating lights lit the interior, and Steve could see people scampering around to windows to see what was happening. Fred was the first one out the door. Exactly six feet tall and a well-proportioned two hundred pounds, Fred was a striking figure in his company's uniform that was reminiscent of the army officer's pinks and greens during the World War II era.

"Most people just knock," he chided Steve.

"Just wanted to make sure everybody was awake."

"You've accomplished your objective. You can turn those strobes off now."

Steve turned off the car's overheads and followed Fred inside. There were three desks in the front office: one for the operations officer, one for the administrative person surrounded by office equipment, and one for Amy. Behind Amy's desk were several computers and copiers. A bank of a dozen radios stood in chargers on the wall beside the operations desk. This wasn't the first time Steve had been in the offices, but he always marveled at how well organized everything was.

Amy came from behind her desk, gave Steve a hug, and led him to the kitchen area where the coffeepot was always on 24/7. Amy was a very attractive lady with auburn hair that rested on her shoulders. When she smiled, her whole face seemed to smile. She enjoyed interacting with people and had taken a liking to Steve early on. Fred and Steve knew that there was a flip side to her personality, though. Get her riled up, and she could verbally cut you up into little pieces. Though only 5'3" tall and a shapely 140 pounds, she would stand toe-to-toe with any man should physical emphasis on a point of contention be necessary.

Steve spent several hours with Fred and Amy, working up a plan to deal with the dilemma that faced both the hospital and the sheriff's office. When he left, Steve was confident that he had a proposal that all three—the sheriff, the hospital administration, and CPI—could live with.

Craig gathered all of the reports concerning the death of Watson and took them to the county attorney's office early Friday morning. He only had to go a short distance down the hall from his office. Sarah Cousins generally got in at or around 9:00 AM, so Craig made sure he was there at that time.

The county attorney was a stout female, broad shouldered and big boned. She appeared to suffer from severe allergies. Her eyes were always bloodshot, and her face was generally flushed. Her voice was rather small and soft for her size. She was removing her over coat when she saw Craig enter the office.

"Tell me you've come to tell me it isn't so," she said to him, pausing with her coat down around her shoulders.

"Hi ya, Sarah. Let me help you with that coat." Craig moved toward her.

"Stop! Don't come any closer until you tell me that what I read in the paper didn't happen."

"Sorry, Sarah," he began, "we lost one of our charges yesterday, and no one feels more responsible than I do."

"You and I have discussed the possibility of something tragic like this happening Craig, but I never really expected it. Tell me what happened." She took a seat at her desk.

Craig put the reports he was carrying on her desk, sat down across from her, and told her the sequence of events. When he had finished, he picked up the reports and handed them to her.

"What happened and what everybody did afterward is in there. The conditions that provided the opportunity for this to happen are on all of our shoulders." He paused and looked her straight in the eyes before continuing." You and I haven't pushed hard enough for changing the conditions in the jail. We've allowed the way we've operated in the past to cloud our vision of the present and the future. We don't have anybody to blame but ourselves."

The ringing phone on Sarah's desk interrupted the conversation. She answered it and was informed by the secretary that Craig's daughter, Katie, was trying to get in touch with him.

"Call your daughter," Sarah said. "There's enough blame to go around, Craig. Our job now is to put this asshole where he belongs and make sure that this sort of thing doesn't happen again."

Craig headed back to his office to return the call to his daughter.

Katie had come home a couple of months ago after giving up on a failed relationship with a guy she met at the bar in the Red Feather. The Red Feather was a popular watering hole for mine and oil management types and some roustabouts. It had a good restaurant and, on weekends, featured live music. In spite of the apprehension and misgivings expressed by her parents, the power of persuasion was too great, and Katie had flown off into the unknown, promising to let her parents know where she was when she got settled in. That was three years ago. The call had come when she could no longer endure the alcoholism, drugs, and physical abuse. She had put aside her pride and asked for her mother's help in getting home from California.

"Hi ya, hon, what's up?" Craig said into the phone.

"Hi, Dad," Katie started. "Mom forgot to tell you that she had to go for a six-month mammogram exam today. So she wanted to make sure you had enough cash to have lunch out someplace."

"I'll be fine. You going with her?"

"Yeah, I'm gonna drive her."

"Thanks, Katie, and good luck."

"Love you, Dad," Katie said before hanging up."

Martha had been getting these checkups regularly since some of her friends had been diagnosed with cancer that could have been caught early had they had mammograms done. Each time she had the checkup, Craig had asked himself what ifs.

What if they say there's evidence of cancer? He never came up with an answer and had never discussed it with Martha. Like always, other things got in the way, such as Steve coming in.

"Hey, boss. Got a minute?" Steve asked, not really waiting for an answer.

"Sure, what's up?"

"Met with CPI this morning, and we've got a deal as long as the contract is with us. The rules and policies they are to follow are ours. They would be happy to cooperate with the hospital staff in any way they can to make things work smoothly. Problems will occur if the nursing staff and doctors impede their ability to provide protection when it's been determined that certain actions need to be taken. They'll also do the transport to other treatment facilities when needed. That sure takes a load off this office."

"Did we get a proposed cost for all this?" Craig asked.

"Yes, sir. They'll put people at the hospital at the rate of $10 a man-hour, per detainee, for as long as they are needed."

"If there should be a need for two guards on a detainee, would that be $10 a man-hour for each of them?"

"Yes, sir," Steve answered.

"What about the cost to transport?"

"$10 per man-hour plus 25 cents a mile."

Craig had taken a small calculator out of his center drawer and began punching in numbers. After a few moments, he looked up at Steve with a look of disbelief on his face.

"If we put a deputy up there, it'll cost us $15.75 a man-hour plus time and a half over time." He paused, punched in some numbers, and continued, "If it's on a weekend, it costs us double time a man-hour. Our mileage costs are three cents more than they'll charge us. How did you manage this?"

"I didn't," Steve tried to explain. "CPI has a number of officers who are working part-time but would like to work more hours. By taking this on, they have a better shot at keeping these people they've already trained until a permanent post comes available. It's a win-win for the SO and CPI."

"When can they start?" Craig asked.

"As soon as the hospital administrator agrees to the procedures," Steve replied.

"How will the notification process be handled?"

"CPI will respond to a call from the jail—Sherrie's office," Steve began. "When CPI gets the call that there's a person going into detention, one of their staff or Fred or Amy will go to the hospital, get briefed by the deputy or police officer making the commitment, determine the gender of guard needed, and, after the emergency room doctor releases the person—with the help of hospital security—secure the individual in the designated detention room. The CPI staff person relieves the hospital security officer, starts the log that will be kept on the detainee, and performs whatever tasks are required until the assigned security officer arrives. They'll run eight-hour shifts until the person is released or transported someplace else."

"Write it up." Craig reached for his phone and dialed Josh's number.

Josh' Secretary answered, "Memorial Hospital, Mr. Betinoli's office."

"Hi ya, doll. This is Craig Spence for Josh. Put him on, would you please?"

"I'm sorry, Sheriff. Mr. Betinoli is out of the office right now. Can I take a message?"

"Yes, find him and have him call me STAT." Craig hung up the phone and turned to Steve.

"Get with the security people up there before the day ends and get this thing pinned down. Now let's go get some lunch. You can drive." Craig reached for his parka. He slammed his cowboy hat on his head and, with Steve hurrying to keep up, strolled down the hall toward the front of the courthouse.

Katie and Martha left the radiology center at Memorial Hospital a little after 1:00 PM and went to the car in the parking lot. With the engine running, to create heat, they sat in the car a long time not saying anything.

The female technician had begun the procedure as usual by standing Martha in front of a machine to which an upper and lower plate was attached. The technician had maneuvered Martha's left breast until she was on her tiptoes and the breast was between the two plates, which were adjusted until they were squishing the breast almost flat. Martha knew it wouldn't do any good to tell her it hurt because it would just prolong the ordeal. Once the plates were in place, the technician went behind a partition and the machine began to make noises. All the while, Martha was thinking, this hurts like hell. No doubt a man designed this. Should have his gonads put between these plates and squashed.

After the right breast had been checked, the technician had Martha relax while she took the X-rays to be reviewed by the radiologist. To Martha's dismay, she returned and had to redo the examination.

When the examination was completed, Martha was allowed to get dressed while the X-rays were being reviewed. After several minutes had passed, she was escorted into a nearby office where a very professional-looking man in a white coat greeted her. On the wall over a desk was an X-ray film stuck into a light panel.

"Mrs. Spence, I'm Dr. Detrick," he began. Before Martha could respond, he continued, "Generally, I'd have you go home, and you'd receive a letter in a few days, letting you know of our findings and giving you further instructions, but I'm a little concerned about what I see on the film."

Taking a pencil, Dr. Detrick pointed to a blurry white splotch on each of the sheets of film. He took a pair of reading glasses from the chest pocket of his white coat and looked closer at the film.

"I would like to make you an appointment with an oncologist to take a look at this film and run some tests," he said.

"Do you have some idea of what's going on?" Martha asked.

"It may be just fibroid tumors," the doctor had responded. "They're generally benign but can be painful. I'm concerned because they weren't there on your last exam."

Martha agreed to an appointment with an oncologist on the following Monday, three days from this visit.

"Going to tell Dad?" Katie broke the silence.

"Of course I am," Martha replied. "The last thing I want to do is keep him in the dark."

"Can he handle it?"

"Katie," Martha softly called out her daughter's name and placed her hand on Katie's arm. "We don't know what the oncologist will find. Let's not start worrying about something we have no control over. If the news is bad, well, let's just wait and see. We'll handle it." Her voice trailed off, and only the sound of the car's heater disturbed the silence. "Let's go home," she said to Katie.

Having put the car in gear, Katie eased it out of the parking lot. A tear began to work its way down her cheek. After wiping it away, she reached over and took her mother's hand in hers.

"Love you, Mom," she said.

Martha squeezed Katie's hand and smiled.

CHAPTER 4

Business at the Rock Springs jail was picking up, and the booking area was buzzing with activity. The sally port door was opening regularly as police officers brought in people from the bars and clubs. Drivers who had gotten an early start on the weekend were being brought in, fingerprinted, had their pictures taken, and were held in the drunk tank until they sobered up. Those who were picked up for fighting, disturbing the peace, or some other misdemeanor offenses were allowed to bail out or be bailed out by family and friends.

Patrol cars pulled into the sally port and were picked up on surveillance cameras mounted on the walls of the building. One of the jail officers pushed a green button under a monitor on the wall behind the booking desk, and the sally port door traveled upward just like a garage door. The patrol officer walked his prisoner in, and an electric eye was activated as they passed through and triggered the door to close.

Lying on his mattress with his head propped against the padded wall, Albert Brown saw the activity and occasionally made comments directed at persons being brought in.

"You sure are an ugly bastard. You need to be locked up!" he had yelled at one drunk.

"Hey, Mr. Policeman, you can put that one in here with me," he called out when an officer brought in a tall buxom female who had been picked up for DUI.

All through the afternoon, he observed the actions of the jail officers, how they handled prisoners when they were being put in and taken out of the cells, and the procedures used when he was allowed to use the toilet in the adjoining cell. He also studied the demeanor of the jailers. They had changed shifts three times since he had been here, and one officer called Muffet worked the midnight shift. He had talked to him, and Muffet had even taken a snooze when things were quiet.

Brown knew that his stay in the city jail was only temporary, and they'd be coming for him as soon as there was a cell at county they could put him in. *One thing for sure,* he thought, *if they get me back in county jail, my goose is cooked.* He got up from his mattress and walked to the bars where he could see what was going on. In his mind, he knew he already wasted too much time.

It was five thirty in the evening and snowing again when Craig crossed the street from the court building to his house. The temperature had dropped considerably since the sun had gone down. He stomped the snow off his boots before going inside.

The front door opened into a large living room that had been furnished with overstuffed couches and armed chairs. An unusually large coffee table sat in front of a brown couch that was adorned with fluffy yellow, green, and tan pillows. A set of French doors opened into the dining room, which was very elegantly furnished. A long walnut table stood in the center with high-backed chairs and China cabinets along the walls.

"Martha, Katie, anybody home?" Craig called out from the dining room.

"We're in the kitchen, Dad," Katie called back.

Before he could reach the door at the end of the room, Martha came through it, wiping her hands with a towel as she came to greet him. He had tossed his hat on the dining room table, reached out and took her face in both hands, gave her a quick kiss on the lips, and then a big hug.

"I love coming home to you, doll," he said as they stood hugging each other.

"I'll remind you of that the next time you get grumpy."

Martha was a very handsome woman with salt-and-pepper hair that she wore cropped just above broad shoulders. She had a round face with large brown eyes that crinkled at the edges when she smiled.

"Glad you're home. I've got dinner ready except for the steaks. By the time you get cleaned up, they'll be ready." She took him by the arm and led him into the kitchen.

Katie was tossing a salad at the kitchen table as Craig made his way to the bathroom just off the kitchen. He leaned over and gave her a peck on the cheek as he passed by.

"Glad you're home, Dad," she said.

It was fairly quiet around the table during dinner. Martha had broiled the steaks to a perfect medium rare, just like Craig liked them, and had included one of Craig's favorite veggie combinations, a baked sweet potato accompanied by sweet peas.

"This is a great meal. You manage to get this steak just right every time, doll. It's perfect."

"When you've had as much practice as I have, eventually, you get it right." Craig and Katie joined Martha in a lighthearted chuckle at her comment.

After Craig had finished eating and Katie had started clearing the dishes, Martha said, "I had the mammogram today," she began. "The doctor is concerned about some blotches he saw during the exam."

Craig reached over for a toothpick from the container in the center of the table. It got quiet in the kitchen except for the clinking of the dishes that Katie was stacking in the dishwasher.

"What does that mean, blotches?" Craig asked.

"There could be some small abnormal tissue growth going on." Martha paused. "They could be small fibroid tumors, or they could be something else."

Craig stopped picking his teeth. The implication of what Martha was saying was beginning to sink in.

Martha reached across the table and took his hand in hers.

"Nothing's for certain yet," she said. "The radiologist wants me to see an oncologist and have some more tests done. I have an appointment this coming Monday. It's my understanding that in women fifty and older, there is a 25 percent chance of a false positive with mammogram interpretations. So let's not jump to conclusions but be prepared to face up to what could be."

Craig walked around the table and, leaning down behind Martha's chair, put his arms around her. Neither of them spoke.

Katie had stopped stacking the dishes and stood with her hands grasping the edge of the counter top. In the window over the sink, she could see the reflection of her mom and dad. There was fullness in her chest, and she couldn't resist the desire to comfort them. With tears streaming down her face, she turned and walked to them. Lifting Craig's right arm, she slid in where she could embrace them both.

Holding Martha with his face pressed into her hair, Craig had prayed. Dear God—a tear began to find its way down his cheek, and his heart was pounding in his chest as his thoughts were with God—*I've only loved three women in my life: my mom, Martha, and my daughter. Please, don't take Martha from me too,* he prayed.

Martha reached up and placed a palm on the cheeks of each of them and spoke softly.

"It'll be okay," she said." We'll get through this. It's just one more bump in the road."

Katie slipped from under Craig's arm and again turned her attention to tidying up the kitchen.

"Why you, doll?" Craig asked as he moved from behind the chair and dropped to one knee so he could look into her face.

"Why not me, Craig?"

"You did everything right. You got the exams religiously—"

"The reason we got those exams was, so we'd catch things early. Now let's let the process play out."

As she got up from the chair, she placed her hand on Craig's head and spoke in a stern voice.

"There'll be enough time for us to feel sorry for ourselves. Now clear out of this kitchen while I help clean up."

He had reluctantly allowed Martha to shoo him off. Now sitting in the great room in his favorite chair, he had let his mind wander back to the past.

He'd met Martha when he and his mother were left with the task of selling the family ranch. Craig's father had died just prior to his seventeenth birthday, after suffering for several years from injuries he got trying to break a wild horse. When he was twenty-one, times were hard, and there was no money, so the decision was made to sell the property and what was left of the stock. Craig would join the military.

Martha had worked in the county clerk's office, where Craig and his mother had to go to search property records. She had helped find all of the appraisal information and spent a great deal of time helping him and his mother understand the terminology used on ownership documents and courthouse filings. One filing caught Mrs. Spence by surprise. The IRS had filed a tax lien against the property several years back. She had never involved herself in the business end of running the ranch.

Martha gave Craig a crash course in the methods used by the IRS. He invited her out to the ranch for dinner to show his appreciation for her help. They began to spend weekends together, horseback riding and picnicking in some of Craig's favorite places, always strategizing and discussing options that might allow the lien to be cleared. Unfortunately, he and his mother had nothing to bargain with, and the IRS was not sympathetic.

The IRS had sold the livestock and property at an auction, and again, Martha came to the rescue. When the lawyer for the new owner, a businessman out of New York State, came to the courthouse to file the sale documents, she found out that there were no plans to occupy the property. She had inquired as to who was going to care for the ranch and was told that the matter would be taken up in a few weeks. She had suggested that the Spences be allowed to stay on as caretakers. The lawyer communicated the suggestion to the new owner, and the

Spence family was hired on. Craig signed up for four years in the navy.

Mrs. Spence passed away after losing the battle with breast cancer. Craig was at sea when it happened, and Martha had worked with the Red Cross to get him back in time for the funeral. While he was home, he and Martha had married.

Craig was still wide awake when the phone rang. The clock on the nightstand showed 3:20. *Not a good sign when the phone rings this early in the morning,* he thought.

"Spence," he said into the phone.

"Sheriff, this is Dispatch. Brown has escaped . . ."

CHAPTER 5

The Saturday night parade of drunks and others that had run afoul of the law had become a trickle. The clock behind the booking desk showed a little after 2:00 AM. The shift had changed at midnight, and Officer Muffet was on duty now. As he was returning from checking one of the other cells, Brown had called out to him.

"Say, Muffet. Can I take a pee?"

"Hold on a minute while I catch up with my log," Muffet had replied.

"You'd better hurry, man. I really gotta go."

Muffet made some entries in his log and then moved over to Brown's cell door.

"Put your hands through the slop shoot," he said. He then placed a set of handcuffs on Brown's wrists, removed a set of keys from his belt, inserted a large-toothed key into the lock, and turned it until there was a loud clunk as the bolt sprung back. Muffet opened the cell door, allowing Brown to come out and walk to the next cell. Brown noticed that Muffet had used the same key to open the door of that cell too.

Just as Muffet was closing the cell door, a buzzer over the sally port had begun to blast, and a red light began to flash. Muffet put the keys on a ring on his belt, ran to the booking desk, and pushed the green button on the wall that activated the big door. As the door opened, two highway patrol officers could be seen wrestling with a mountain of a man with his hands restrained with plastic ties.

All three were on the ground, one officer riding the prisoner's legs as he kicked and pulled with his legs. The other officer was hanging on for dear life with a headlock that was ineffective.

"We could use a little help out here!" one of the officers had called out. "Hit him with the spray!"

Muffet had taken a pepper spray canister from his belt and directed a blast at the big man. The officer with the headlock got it full in the face, and it forced him to release his hold. The big guy then rolled over and pulled free of the officer at his legs. Muffet grabbed the restrained wrists and, pushing the arms upward, forced the man to bend forward, and Muffet drove him headfirst inside. The door began to close, and the two officers barely made it in.

With a mighty grunt, the man snapped the plastic ties, and all four men slammed against the cell door where Brown was. As they struggled, Muffet was pushed against the cell bars. The keys were within reach, and Brown lifted them from the ring. One of the officers delivered a vicious kick to the side of the big man's knee. He cried out and went down on all fours. Muffet and the two officers dragged him across the booking area and down the cell block.

As they dragged the big man across the booking area floor, Brown saw his chance. He reached through the bars, slipped the big key in the lock, and unlocked the door. He lost no time going to the desk and pushing the green button. The door began to open, and he slid through the opening. He sprinted away from the building's security lights and disappeared into the darkness.

By the time he heard the first siren, Brown had used Muffet's cuff key to remove his handcuffs. He had wound his way through alleys and backyards until he came to a large storm drain. He crawled until his knees hurt, and he stopped to rest. For the first time, he felt the cold. The sandals on his feet weren't much for running or keeping the toes warm, and the jail's jumpsuit didn't provide any warmth. He had begun to shiver, so he'd decided to keep moving.

The culvert emptied into a dry creek bed just outside a fenced-in pipe yard. In the glare of security lights mounted on telephone poles, he could see a construction trailer in the yard. He found a place where coyotes and other varmints had crawled under the fence and slithered into the pipe yard.

The pipe yard was at the far west end of town, and there were no houses around, just commercial buildings where no one would be this time of morning. He stayed still for a few moments, looking around. Sirens had stopped; things were almost too quite. *I need to get in that trailer quick,* he thought.

His luck was holding out. When he turned the handle on the door to the trailer, it came open. He slipped inside and stayed low to the floor so that he couldn't be seen through the windows. In the light from the outside, he could see tables with large sheets of paper hanging over the edges. There was a small room at one end of the trailer, and Brown saw a white sink through the open door. On the wall next to what appeared to be a toilet hung a set of construction-type coveralls. He glanced around in the dim lighting and saw a refrigerator and an electric floor heater.

Checking the refrigerator first, he found a Kentucky Fried Chicken box with two pieces of chicken in it and a half-eaten Subway sandwich and a couple of bottles of pop. He took out the chicken and sat with his back against the fridge and ate it. His eyes adjusted to the dim lighting, and he could see a clock on the wall at the far end of the trailer. It was 5:40. He had no idea how long he'd been on the run.

He took down the coveralls and put them on over the jumpsuit. There was even a hood that he put over his head. On the floor where the coveralls were hanging was a pair of lace-up muck locks. He carried them over to the floor heater, turned it on, and laid the boots on their sides so the heat would go inside.

A sudden burst of light through one of the front windows startled him so badly he nearly stuck his foot into the heater coils. His heart was racing. The light had moved from one window to the other, swung away, and then moved along the front of the trailer and through the windows again. Just as quickly as it had come, it was gone. Brown crawled to a window to peer out. There was a patrol car spotlighting around all the buildings and parking lots in the area. He had watched the cars' taillights until they disappeared out of his view.

Boy, that scared the piss out of me, he thought. He went into the room with the toilet and, while relieving himself, noticed a large first-aid kit on the wall. He found Band-Aids, elastic wraps, and iodine. He sat in front of the heater, treating the cuts and scrapes on his feet. When he was ready to move on, he'd use the wraps as socks and put on the boots. He decided that he'd move on after nightfall. He stretched out on the floor to get some much-needed sleep.

It took a moment for the dispatcher's words to register with Craig.

"What?" he exclaimed as he swung his feet to the floor.

"Brown's gone," had come the reply.

"When?" he asked.

"The officer at the Rock Springs Police Department said that he got away just a little bit ago," the dispatcher replied.

"What's being done?" Craig was now pulling on his pants, and Martha was sitting up in bed. She knew it was something big if Craig was getting up.

"SO2 is in route to pick you up," the dispatcher said. "There are two highway patrolmen tracking on foot, and roadblocks are being set up on I-80 and all roads leading out of town."

"Get a hold of Chief Kessler and have him meet us at the city jail," Craig instructed.

"What's wrong?" Martha asked when he hung up the phone.

"The prisoner that we were holding in the Rock Springs City Jail is gone."

"You be careful," Martha cautioned.

A beam of light flashed across the bedroom window. Craig knew that Steve was there to pick him up. He leaned down, gave Martha a peck on the forehead, and hurried out to the car. When Craig got in, Steve was on the radio with the patrol deputies.

"SO10, this SO2, what's your 10-20?" Steve was asking.

"SO10, west side of Rock Springs on Highway 91 at the truck stop."

"This is SO2. Move into that industrial complex on that side of town and check that area."

"10-4, SO2," the patrol deputy had replied.

After Craig had settled into his seat, Steve contacted the other deputy on patrol.

"SO9, this is SO2."

"SO9, go ahead."

"SO9, set up on that service road that runs along the railroad tracks west of town and keep an eye out."

"SO9, 10-4, SO2," the deputy acknowledged.

"Howdy, boss," Steve greeted Craig as he pulled out into the street and headed toward Rock Springs. "This is not good."

"Seems like we're just snakebit," Craig commented. "Have Dispatch call in all off-duty people. I want to form a circle of surveillance that covers most of the city perimeter. I'm sure Chief Kessler is taking care of the inner city."

Craig had taken a map of the county from the glove compartment and began to draw circles where his men had been directed to go.

"One thing's for sure," Craig began. "He's holding up somewhere. It's cold enough to freeze a man in short order."

"That's in our favor, boss," Steve said. "If he's found a place to keep warm, he's still in the area."

"How are we set up for surveillance?" Craig asked.

"We've got every available person, including city officers either patrolling or positioned in places where they can detect movement."

"That'll help keep him bottled up during the day, but it's not going to help us much in the dark," Craig said with a hint of frustration in his voice.

At the city jail, Craig greeted Chief Kessler with a big handshake.

"What's this I hear you've got an unplanned vacancy, Matt?" Craig quipped as he put his arm around Matt Kessler's shoulders.

Chief Kessler was a short, squat-built man with white hair and a reddish-gray handlebar mustache that he stroked as he responded to Craig's query.

"Don't understand it, Spence," he said, sounding a little perplexed. "We offer all the amenities of any Cross Bar Hotel."

"Must be your customer service," Craig joshed.

"That's what happens when you're undermanned," Matt said as he led Craig to the squad room where there was a strong aroma of coffee.

"All we can do is hope that the cold weather makes him hunker down someplace," Craig said as the chief poured him a cup of coffee. "The downside," he continued after taking a sip, "he might break into somebody's house, hold them hostage, or steal their car, or, worse yet, force them to drive him off." Craig took another sip of his coffee before continuing. "What happened, Matt?"

Craig listened intently as the chief explained the series of events as he had gotten them from Officer Muffet. While he was telling the story, a call came through on the handheld radio he carried.

"Rock Springs PD, this is WHP Six Zero," the voice was saying.

The conversation between Craig and Matt stopped as they both listened for what the Wyoming Highway Patrolman would have to say.

"WHP Six Zero, PD Dispatch."

"WHP Six Zero on foot, five hundred block, Third Street, found set of keys behind garage at 512 Third. Looks like they might belong to you."

"This is Dispatch. Do they have what looks like a key to the cell doors?

"That's affirmative."

Matt keyed the mike attached to the shirt lapel of his left shoulder and interrupted the transmission.

CHAPTER 6

"Six Zero, Rock Springs One. Stand by that area, would ya? I'll have some people meet you there."

"10-4, Chief," came the reply.

While Matt busied himself getting his people out to where the keys had been found, Craig had contacted his dispatch and had a call placed to the penitentiary in Rawlins to see if he could borrow one of their tracking dogs. He knew that Brown had nothing to lose, so the possibility that he might hurt someone was probable. He wanted to be hot on his tail and minimize the risk.

Steve had come to the squad room, and Craig could hear the dispatcher on Steve's radio.

"—are on field trials in Colorado," Craig could hear her say.

"10-4, Dispatch," Steve acknowledged, ending the conversation.

"What was that all about?" Craig asked.

"No dogs available, boss. They're on some type of field training down in Colorado."

"I tell you we're snakebit!" Craig exclaimed, banging his fist on the table and knocking over his coffee. "Crap!" he exclaimed. "After I clean this up, let's go see what Matt's got."

CHAPTER 7

A little after midnight, CPI got its first call from the sheriff's office to secure a detained person at the hospital. The station master at the bus station had requested assistance, removing a male party from the premises.

Two Rock Springs PD officers that responded and found a young man in the men's room charging the door of one of the stalls like a bull. The officers had watched as he hit the door with his head, backed off, and charged the door again, all the while letting out a groan—"Unnnnnnnnnnnnuh!"—that would end when his head hit the door. After witnessing the third charge, the officers intervened.

One of the officers placed himself in front of the stall door as the man prepared for another charge. The other had gotten behind him, ran his baton under the man's belt, grabbed the back of his jacket collar with his other hand, and lifted the lower end of the baton. The man was forced upon his tiptoes. With the tip of the baton putting pressure in the middle of his back and unable to plant his feet on the floor, the officer was able to force and hold him against the wall while the other officer put cuffs on him.

The man's face was full of blood from wounds on his forehead. His long black hair was stuck to his face, glued there by the coagulating blood. As the officers moved him out of the station to the waiting squad car, he had begun to grind his teeth and make strange clicking sounds with his tongue against the roof of his mouth. A safety pat down had produced several plastic inserts, the type that wallets have for cards and pictures. A social security card, a picture of an elderly couple, and a student ID card issued by Louisiana State University was all that was in them. Nothing else was in his pockets.

The information gathered from the items, his name—Norman Cretin—and social, was run through the National Crime Information Center (NCIC), and he came back as a missing person being sought by the authorities in Louisiana.

At the hospital, two hospital security officers met the two PD officers, and the four of them had not been able to dislodge Norman from the backseat of the police car. He had lashed out with his feet at anyone who came close and tried to bite anyone that grabbed him. Without warning, Norman just dove out of the car onto the pavement where a security officer tackled him. Three officers held Norman down while one of the security officers had gone for a gurney.

Norman was placed, kicking and screaming, on the gurney and secured to it with leather restraints at the ankles, his wrists, and across his midsection. It was obvious that he was a danger to himself or others, so the sheriff's office was advised that long-term security would be needed.

Fred Dreskel arrived at the hospital after Norman had been rolled into an exam room where an emergency room doctor would examine him, have his wounds dressed, and then release him to go to a lockup room.

Fred was being briefed by the police officers when the doctor came into the room. He was very thin, and his white coat was much too big for him. He had fiery-red hair and freckles.

"I won't examine him all trussed up like that," he said. "Take those restraints off him."

Norman was grinding his teeth again, and he had a wild look in his eyes. His breathing had become rapid, and his legs were twitching.

"I don't think you want to do that, Doc," Fred cautioned. Experience was telling him that there was an eruption building up here.

"I just won't examine him like that," the doctor repeated his refusal.

The hospital security officers, intimidated by the status doctors enjoy in the hospital, began to remove the restraints. Fred and the two PD officers watched in disbelief. The restraints came off one by one, first the right wrist, then the right ankle, the left wrist, and the left ankle. As the strap across Norman's midsection was removed, the doctor moved in to examine the wounds on Norman's forehead.

"How'd he get these?" he had asked, referring to the head wounds.

Had there been an answer, the doctor wouldn't have heard it. Norman went ballistic. He came up off the gurney, uttering a blood-curdling scream, catching the doctor right in the teeth with a head butt. The doctor went down, and Norman was right on top of him, screaming into his face. Everyone reacted and freed the doctor from Norman's grip. The restraints were put back on, and the doctor, bleeding from his lower lip, had to be helped out of the room by Fred. A nurse finished the job on Norman's forehead, and Fred, along with one of the security officers, pushed the gurney through the hallways to the detention room.

It was a modified patient room. There was a door leading in from the hallway with an eight by four observation window in it. The door could only be opened from the outside. A bathroom with a shower off to one side and then another door with the same-sized observation window led into the room. Inside the room, all electrical outlets were covered, and there were no light switches. Lights were controlled from the hallway. A large window looked out on the hospital lawn. Double heavy-gauged Plexiglas let the light in and resisted attempts to escape.

Fred positioned the gurney in the middle of the room so that the officer he assigned to guard Norman would be able to see him through the observation windows without entering the room. The officer would check on him every fifteen or twenty minutes. Norman would remain in restraints until the doctor that would be assigned to emergency detainees by the hospital saw him.

A train passing in the distance blowing its horn had brought Brown wide awake with a start. Looking out of one of the back windows, he could see a freight train making its way east through Rock Springs. He had wished he were closer to those tracks so he could hitch a ride. The sun was going down, and he needed to decide what he was going to do. Looking out of the front windows, he could see traffic moving along a road in front of the pipe yard. Watching the passing cars, he noticed that they turned either left or right just up the road about half a mile. Those that turned left seemed to just head out into desert country. That was where he'd go tonight. Less chance of running into the cops.

He had been walking along a paved road for what seemed like hours. The night sky was clear, and the moon was out. He had watched the sun go down, so he figured he was walking south. He just knew he had to stay out of sight until he got somewhere. He had seen nothing along this road but prairie, rocky hills of pinion trees, and an occasional coyote run across the road. The muck locks he'd put on were way too big. Walking was hard, but his feet were warm, and the coveralls were so well insulated that he had to unzip the front and let some cold air in.

Up ahead, he saw what appeared to be a beam of light. He stopped walking and watched for a few moments. He could barely make out the outline of a car. Moving closer, he realized the light was coming from a flashlight, and someone was working under the hood.

He moved as close as he dared, sat down behind a pinion, and waited. When the person got in the car and started it, Brown moved up, squatted beside the car, and picked up a rock from the side of the road. When the man came out to put the hood down, he lunged and struck the surprised man in the ribs with the rock. There was a scream, and the man had started to fall. As he

was going down, Brown struck out again, bringing the rock down on the side of the falling man's head.

A woman came running from the back of a U-Haul trailer that was hooked to the car. When she saw what had happened, she screamed and tried to get to the injured man. Brown grabbed her, threw her to the ground, and wrapped his hands around her throat. The more she fought and kicked, the harder he squeezed until she went limp.

The man was on his feet, stumbling and falling toward him. Brown had seen a toolbox by the right front wheel of the car. He moved in a wide arc around the man, who was now on all fours. He reached in the toolbox and grabbed a large screwdriver. With both hands, he drove the screwdriver into the man's body where the neck and shoulder met. There was an agonizing scream, and Brown repeatedly kicked the man alongside the head until there was no sound and no further movement.

Brown picked up the flashlight, stuck it in the leg pocket of the coveralls, and dragged the woman's lifeless body to the U-Haul. He used the flashlight to see what was inside. There was furniture, lamps, lots of boxes, some cloths hanging on the trailer wall, and a mattress lying flat on the trailer floor where nothing had been stacked. He laid the body on the mattress.

In the distance, Brown had seen the glare of headlights. There was a rise on the road, and the glare was gradually lighting up more of the countryside. He hurried to get the man onto the floor between the backseat and the front seats. An eighteen-wheeler topped the knoll, and Brown stood beside the car with his hand on his crotch as if he were taking a pee, he waved as the truck roared by and the trucker blew his horn.

The key was still in the switch, and the engine cranked right up when he turned it. In the light from the dash, he could see things on the passenger seat. Using the flashlight, he saw a wallet, an Arizona Cardinals cap, and a handgun. The handgun was a Glock 9 mm, and it had a full clip in it. The wallet had a couple of credit cards, an Arizona driver's license, some pictures, and several twenty-dollar bills.

Brown pulled the car onto the road. He was headed north back to Rock Springs. *Maybe they won't be expecting me to be coming into town,* he thought as the car began to pick up speed. The clock on the dash said 11:45, and the display showed that there was a quarter of a tank of gas left.

Just before getting to Rock Springs, there was a mass of flashing red lights.

"Damn it! Roadblock!" Brown said out loud. *Too late to stop now,* he thought, *and turning around ain't happening with this trailer.* He put the handgun in the leg pocket of the coveralls. He put his right hand in the pocket and drove with his left.

"If this is it, this is it," he said softly aloud as he wrapped his hand around the weapon, leaving it in the pocket.

As he approached the patrol cars blocking the road, he saw an opening between cars in his lane. Just as he had made up his mind to crash through, an officer stepped out from behind one of the cars and was waving him through. The on-ramp to I-80 east was just beyond the roadblock, and he took it.

After traveling a couple of miles, Brown saw a flying-J sign and decided this was as good a time as ever to get some gas. There were four islands with pumps, so he took the one farthest from the building, the one that truckers used. He locked the car and went into the U-Haul. He took off the coveralls and put on a wool shirt, some jeans and a blue parka that were hanging on the trailer wall. After locking the doors to the U-Haul, he walked in to the cashier and prepaid for $20 worth of gas. It only took $18 worth, but he didn't go for his change.

The guy on the floor in the back was beginning to move around and moan. Brown began to panic. He crawled into the backseat and struck him three times with the butt of the gun. The man was quiet, and he was bleeding pretty good from a gash on his head. He'd have to get rid of him, Brown thought as he pulled back onto I-80 and headed east.

CHAPTER 8

Craig had spent a long night about the town of Rock Springs and had arrived at home just in time to grab a cup of coffee before leaving with Katie and Martha for the oncologist's office. He had been asleep in the backseat of the car when Katie parked in front of the building marked, "UNIVERSITY CANCER INSTITUTE."

When Katie turned off the car's engine, Martha had reached back to wake Craig.

"We're here," she said, tugging on his jacket. "You want to stay here and sleep, or are you coming in with us?"

"I'm coming, I'm coming," Craig had said sleepily as he sat up, stretching his arms.

They walked down the hallway to the oncologist's office. At the receptionist desk, a chubby young lady checked a roster and found Martha's name, handed her a clipboard full of forms, and told her to fill out all the forms where there were items highlighted.

The waiting area was filled with men and women. Craig had seen that some were obviously in various stages of treatment because most of the women were wearing an array of head coverings, and he could see that there was no hair in the back of their heads below the baseball caps that some wore.

After turning the clipboard over to the receptionist, the three of them were led to another waiting room. This one was more private. There was a table with six chairs and a phone. They had seated themselves, Craig and Martha on one side of the table and Katie on the other, when a tall female in white medical coat entered the room. She had short blonde hair, wore thick glasses that magnified her eyes, and smiled warmly as she took a seat at the end of the table nearest Martha. Her name tag read, "Penny Mott MD-Oncology."

"I'm Dr. Mott," she said. "Which of you is Martha?"

"I am," Martha spoke up.

"And the rest of you are?"

"I'm Craig, her husband," Craig had said as he reached out to shake her hand, "and this is our daughter, Katie."

"I'm very glad to meet each of you," Dr. Mott said as she opened a folder that she had placed on the table in front of her. "Martha, I've been assigned your case," she continued. "I want to review the results of your biopsy with you."

Martha had taken Craig's hand in her left hand, and Katie had reached across and put both hands on theirs.

Dr. Mott reached out and took Martha's right hand before continuing. "The tissue tested positive," she said. "That's the bad news," she continued. "But there's good news. We caught it early, and we have treatment options."

Craig was not prepared for the diagnosis even though he had always known that it could turn out this way. The tears welled up in his eyes, and he could feel Katie's hand tighten on his. He looked up and saw her wiping tears from her face. Martha removed her hand from theirs, took some tissues from her purse, and dabbed at her eyes. She had been the first to speak.

"What are my options?" The strength that was usually in her voice had been noticeably absent.

"I'll need to run some additional tests before making any recommendations, but there is surgery, chemo, radiation, or combinations of each," Dr. Mott explained.

The Spence family spent the next thirty minutes or so questioning the doctor about the effectiveness of each of the treatment options, the side effects, and the length of time that Martha would be undergoing treatment.

"When could we get the treatment started?" Craig had asked, showing his anxiousness.

"I'd like to order some labs today. We can draw the blood and take some more pictures. Then you can go home, and I'll be in contact with you in couple of days. At that point, we can discuss the options, and together we can choose the route that might be most effective."

It was late when they left the hospital. The tops of the snow-covered mountains surrounding Salt Lake City were orange and multishades of egg yolk yellow as they reflected the setting sun that no longer bathed the valley floor with its warmth. The air was crisp as they walked to the car. Martha and Katie wrapped their arms around each other's waist while Craig went ahead, hands in his pockets and his cowboy hat pushed to the back of his head. No one spoke until they reached the car.

"I'll drive," Craig announced, holding out his hand for the keys.

"Didn't like my driving coming up here?" Katie was trying to be lighthearted.

"Not that," Craig began. "The traffic is going to be horrific until we hit Park City, and I'd just soon be driving."

In the past few years, Park City, Utah, had evolved from a high-mountain community of sparsely spaced million-dollar chalets and dirt roads to million-dollar chalets, multimillion-dollar condominium complexes, well-engineered asphalt streets, and the premiere ski resort in the state of Utah. Katie hadn't noticed much of the off-highway scenery as she drove into Salt Lake and her last remembrance of the area was from several years back. She had taken a seat in the back of the car, so she was able to take in the views from both sides of the highway.

The traffic was heavy. Craig checked the dash clock, and it was ten before six, the tail end of the peak evening rush hour he surmised. The inside lanes of the highway had snow patches where the blades of snowplows didn't get down to the asphalt, but that didn't cause the traffic to slow down. Craig chose to stay in the outside or slow lane. The posted speed limit was sixty-five and he was cruising at fifty-five.

"I really appreciate you being cautious," Martha said, breaking the silence. "It's been a long day, and I'm a little on the edge."

"I had begun to think that if they took any more blood from you, I'd have to give you some of mine," Craig said. "I think they took seven or eight vials, and that's enough to make anybody a little shaky."

"The worst part was the waiting," Martha complained. "No one seemed to be ready for me, and then at every test, there were the same questions. What's your name? Martha Spence, I'd say. What's your birth date? October 2, 1929, I'd say. It was written on the wristband and on all the papers. I began to get irritated."

"They just don't want to make a mistake and treat the wrong patient for the wrong thing, "Craig assured her.

"You mean they might mix me up with a prostate cancer patient?"

Craig laughed so hard that if there had been some place to do so, he would have pulled off the road. Katie was in the backseat, squealing and clapping her hands like a little girl. It felt good to laugh. It released a lot of the tension brought on by the day's stresses.

However, the glee was short lived. A pickup truck was doing 360s up ahead, and vehicles following were all over the road, giving lots of room for it to do its dance. Craig pulled as far to the roadside as he could and stopped the car. Smoke was coming from the pickup's rear tires as it seemed to spin in slow motion, once, twice, three times, and as they watched in amazement, it finally spun into the median and stopped.

"All's well that ends well," Craig said to Martha and Katie as they watched. Headlights from other vehicles illuminated the people that got out of the truck and walked around it. Those same lights also reflected off the black ice that lined the tracks made by earlier traffic. Craig, recognizing the potential for others to slide into cars, stopped on the road and carefully maneuvered his way back into the outside lane behind an eighteen-wheeler that had just eased by. He decided to stay tucked in behind the truck until road conditions improved.

Martha and Katie had been very quiet since the pickup episode. They both were being respectful of Craig's need to concentrate and pay attention to what was going on around them. Katie was the first to break the silence.

"That has to be scary when you lose control like that, huh, Dad?"

"You don't really have time to be scared while it's happening. You're busy trying to keep the ass end from catching up with the front, trying to slow down the rotation, or just hanging on in an effort not to overreact and flip over," Craig replied.

"I'm glad you were driving when we saw that. I know I would have freaked out and tried to stop," Katie said.

"That's what generally happens, and you end up with a bunch of cars piled on top of one another," Martha chimed in.

The truck in front of them had picked up speed, and loose snow was billowing up behind it, causing zero visibility at times. Craig slowed the car until they were out of the swirling snow and visibility was better. Taking advantage of an opportunity, he changed lanes and gradually eased his way pass the truck. The road was clear of ice now, and the traffic was moving at the posted speed limit of sixty-five miles an hour.

"What did the two of you think of Dr. Mott?" Martha asked.

"I thought she was very professional. She didn't try to give us any false hope, and at the same time, she didn't make me feel that we didn't have a chance to beat this," Craig responded.

"I was too busy listening to what she was saying. Don't really have an opinion one way or the other," Katie remarked. "How about you, Mom?"

"For some reason, I felt very comfortable with her," Martha said. Continuing, she said, "Maybe it was because she didn't make me feel like, 'Oh, you poor thing.'" Turning in her seat so she could look at Katie, she asked, "You know what I mean?"

"Guess so," Katie answered.

Craig could hear Martha and Katie talking to each other, but he really wasn't paying attention to what they were saying. There was a Greyhound bus ahead, and he began to wonder who might be on it that would end up in detention at the hospital. Since he and Josh had come to an agreement, there had been five emergency detentions in just a couple of days. He recalled the last report the office got from CPI.

At nine forty on Saturday night, CPI had gotten a call from Sherrie, his jail administrator, that there was a person being admitted to the hospital that would be detained for her own protection. According to the report, a Greyhound bus traveling east on I-80 had come upon a female lying in the fetal position in the middle of the eastbound lanes west of Green River. As the bus had approached, she had straightened out a leg. Realizing that she was alive, the driver stopped and positioned the bus so that others would not strike her. It was cold, and the wind was blowing; so with the help of a passenger, the female was placed on the bus and taken to the bus depot in Rock Springs, where the bus was met by the Rock Springs Police Department and the female was taken to the emergency room.

When CPI's guard arrived, she had already been placed in lockup and was walking around the room, singing religious songs. Periodically, she would stop, drop to her knees, and appear to be praying. Under the watchful eye of the female guard, the detained person continued to walk the room and pray throughout the night. When the priest, a man in his eighties, made his rounds in the morning and was let into the room to visit with her, she began to scream.

"He's raping me! He's raping me!"

The poor priest had wheeled around and hurried out of the room. His faced flushed, and he was so short of breath that the guard had sat him in her chair and called a nurse to check on him.

The female reacted in the same manner when the doctor came to evaluate her. He too felt it best to observe her from outside the room. He decided to keep her under observation for the full period allowed and give the security people and nurses an opportunity to try meaningful communications with her.

When nurses had come to take her vital signs, she answered all questions with incoherent responses.

"Could you tell me your name?" the nurse had asked.

"Behold, I stand before you as I am, and he called me Mary," was the reply.

"Is Mary your name?"

"When I hear him call my name, I shall answer his call."

"Where do you live, Mary?" the nurse continued to probe.

"I shall reside in the house of the Lord forever."

The nurse continued asking pertinent questions throughout the examination but made no headway in obtaining an identification or information that would make some sense of why she was where she was found.

Late into the night, when the security officer was making a welfare check, Mary asked, "Could I please have some water?"

The officer had a plastic container of ice water at her station. She delivered a Styrofoam cup of water and waited patiently while Mary, taking several big gulps, drank the whole thing.

"Bless you," she said as she handed back the cup and proceeded to lie down on a mattress.

According to the security officer's report, Mary had remained lucid for a short time during which she said that she had come from California in a truck that had given her a ride. She and the driver had prayed together, and then he had thrown himself upon her and taken from her what she had not wished to give. When she was asked where she was going, Mary again began to recite what sounded like scripture, curled up on her mattress, and slept.

The decision to hire on the security company had already proven to be a good one. Craig spent the rest of the trip home, going over the events of the last seventy-two hours in his mind. There had been five involuntary commitments to the detention section at the hospital, Brown had escaped from the city jail, and every able-bodied deputy was on the street, trying to track him down. *Without that security company, there's no way I'd be able to hold up my end of the deal with Josh,* he thought.

CHAPTER 9

At 6:30 AM the next day, the dispatcher at the SO received a telephone call from a woman at Point of Rocks, a small settlement of mobile homes and camper trailers thirty-five miles east of Rock Springs. The woman was calling from the restaurant-gas station. She had said that she wanted to report a man buried alive in the desert.

"Any SO unit, Dispatch, give your 10-20." (Give your location) The call had gone out over the air.

"SO5, Green River," was the first response received.

"SO7, White Mountain Road," came the second.

"SO6, Arrow Head, south of Rock Springs," came the third.

The dispatcher could see on the wall map that SO6 was closest to Point of Rocks.

"SO6," she said, "see the woman at Point of Rocks restaurant. Reports man buried alive."

There was a long pause. Then SO6 came back.

"Dispatch, SO6, 10-9?" (Say again)

"SO6, I say again. See the woman at Point of Rocks restaurant. Reports man buried alive."

"10-4, Dispatch," responded the deputy. "Have a detective meet me there. I'm in route."

"10-4, SO6," acknowledged the dispatcher.

The woman explained that she and her friend exercise every morning by walking in the desert. This morning, as they crossed a dry sandy creek bed, the ground had begun to move. Both women froze and stared at the spot. It was like in the movies, where the dead come out of their graves. First, a hand had come up out of the sand. Then an arm had come out. They started to back away and, as if a signal had been given, began to run back the way they'd come. Stumbling, huffing, and puffing between screams, they were almost back to the highway when they stopped and convinced each other to go back. Cautiously, they had approached the spot. There was moaning, and the arm was trying to push the sand away. Both women had gotten on their knees and pushed at the sand and saw that there was a young man under there. The man's upper torso was full of dried blood. Realizing he was hurt bad; one woman had gone back to the restaurant and told the owner. When he heard what she'd found, he'd called the Sweetwater Power Plant for an ambulance. The medical team from the Power Plant had transported the man to Memorial Hospital before SO6 got there.

Kevin Marcy walked into the restaurant while the deputy was still listening to the women tell their story. He listened intently until the deputy introduced him.

"Betty Clause and Christine Rawls, this is detective Kevin Marcy," he said as he pulled up a chair from another table. "These are the ladies that found the man buried in the sand."

Kevin took out a small notebook and a pen from his jacket pocket. He directed his question at both women.

"While you were walking and before you found the person, did you see anything unusual out there?"

Betty, a middle-aged woman who wore her dirty blonde hair in a ponytail that stuck through the back of a baseball cap, had been the one to speak up.

"No," she said. "It was just a normal morning, nothing different or unusual."

"Was there anyone else out and about that you saw?" Kevin pressed on.

"No, no one but us," Betty answered again.

"How about you, Christine? What did you see?"

Christine was a heavy middle-aged woman. She wore a fur hat with flaps that covered her ears and a sheep-wool-lined parka that was almost too small.

"Nothing unusual," Christine responded. "Just the guys going to work like they do every morning. They stop here, pick up coffee and a six-pack, and head out to the plant or the mine."

"What time was it, Christine?" Kevin asked.

"We left my camper right at six o'clock, so it was a little after six when we walked past the restaurant here. Then we walked up the side of the highway a little ways before cutting into the desert."

"Betty," Kevin inquired, "when you dug the guy out, did he say anything?"

"He was mostly moaning. He was in pretty bad shape."

"Did you hear him say anything, Christine?"

"I stayed while Betty came back to the restaurant," she said. "He kept mumbling something that sounded like mother, but I couldn't make head nor tails of it.

Kevin turned to the deputy and instructed him to speak with the owner and get the names of the people that he knew had stopped in here this morning. He went to the pay phone on the restaurant wall and called the sheriff's office. He spoke with Steve Lolly, related the story that he had been told, and asked Steve to get someone to the hospital and see if they could speak to the guy before he expired. He then turned to the women and had them show him where they had found the man.

The scene was a mess. People's tracks were all over the place going in all directions. Kevin notified the SO dispatch by radio that there was a need for crime scene security and asked that she contact CPI.

The hole that the women pointed out to Kevin was very shallow. The frost line was about twelve to eighteen inches from the top. Whoever had tried to bury this guy had only been able to scoop out the top ten or so inches and then shove the sand over the body.

Steve Lolly got to the hospital at 7:45 AM and was told by the power plant medical team that the individual was in surgery, and that one of his wounds was life threatening.

"Were you able to talk to him on the way in?" Steve asked the EMT.

"Not really. He was in and out. He did keep saying something about his mother being hurt."

"Was he in an accident?" Steve asked.

"Don't know. Didn't see anything on the way in."

"Where was he hurt?"

"He had one bad puncture wound at the base of the neck at the left shoulder, a gash on the right side of the head, and bruises on the face," the EMT replied.

"Think he'll make it?" Steve had asked.

"He lost a lot of blood. Depends on whether we got him here in time or not."

Craig got back to his office at approximately 3:00 PM. Sherrie Munson briefed him on the events of the day and the status of the search for Brown. She told him that the highway patrol had dismantled all roadblocks at noon, and it's assumed that Brown slipped out of town somehow. She also let him know that the man discovered partially buried out at Point of Rocks was in ICU at the hospital, and Steve was standing by to talk to him as soon he was able. CPI is securing the scene where the man was found, and Kevin is handling that part of the investigation she told him. "Why does my gut tell me that there is a connection between the Point of Rocks deal and Albert Brown?" Craig wondered out loud.

"Steve and Kevin feel that there may be a second person connected to the victim found in the sand," Sherrie volunteered. "According to the women who found him and the ambulance crew, he kept muttering something about his mother."

The phone had interrupted their conversation. Sherrie answered it.

"Munson here," she said. "Hold on, I'm putting you on speaker." She pushed the speaker button, then said," Okay, go ahead, Steve."

"I just finished speaking with Stacey Cappers, the guy found buried out at Point of Rocks," Steve announced. "He and his mother were traveling along Highway 91 Sunday evening pulling a U-Haul trailer when their car, a 1979 white Lincoln Continental, blew a vacuum hose. He had just fixed it when some guy in insulated coveralls attacked him. It was dark, and he didn't get a good look at his face. He was knocked to the ground and then stabbed with something, and he blacked out for some time. He remembers regaining consciousness and seeing his mother being dragged to the back of the trailer. He tried to go to her, and that's all he remembers. He believes that they were only a few miles south of I-80, traveling north when the car lost power"

"Did he tell you about what was in the car and the trailer?" Craig asked.

"Yeah, that's the bad part," Steve said. "He had a handgun in the car. His wallet had a couple hundred dollars, he thinks. In the trailer were furniture, a mattress that his mother slept on while he drove, and some changes of clothes."

"Anything else that we can use?" Craig had asked.

"No, he sort of drifted off, and the doctors shooed me out."

"Okay," Craig said. "I'll get out an all points with what we have to everybody east of here."

Sherrie had been taking notes during the conversation and was ready to pass them on to the dispatcher. She paused a moment and queried Craig.

"What's the verdict on Martha's condition?" she asked.

"The tests were positive," Craig answered.

"Damn! Why do bad things always happen to good people?" Sherrie asked rhetorically as she had walked around the desk and placed her hand on his shoulder.

"We've got a couple of days to decide what treatment to go with," Craig informed her as they both headed toward the dispatch area.

Both Craig and Sherrie helped the dispatcher construct the all-points bulletin. After it was aired, Sherrie shared a concern with Craig.

"Sheriff," she began, "until we corral this guy Brown, I'd sure feel better if we placed a guard on Stacey Cappers."

"Great idea," Craig agreed. "Get CPI to put an armed guard on him as long as he's in the hospital or until we get Brown off the street."

Back at his desk, Craig began to develop a plan for continued efforts aimed at catching up to Brown. He knew that he had to cover a wide area with information. All of Wyoming, Utah, and Colorado needed to be in on this. The first step was getting the all-points bulletin out to law enforcement agencies. Now the public needed to be made aware of what he was looking for. He began to make a list of all newspapers, radio, and TV stations that he could think of. He also made another list of the things he suspected was connected to Brown's movements.

Craig was pretty certain that the assault that happened out on Highway 91 had been Brown's handy work. The victim hadn't mentioned an orange jumpsuit, but he did say his attacker was wearing insulated coveralls. If it was Brown, he probably broke in someplace and shed his jail suit.

Craig picked up the phone and pushed the button that would connect him to the dispatcher.

"Dispatch," he said, "did we get any calls about break-ins this morning?"

"Yeah, Sheriff," the dispatcher responded. "There were three burglary calls and a couple of theft reports."

"What were the locations of the theft reports?" Craig asked.

"One was at Whistland Chevrolet and the other was at the offices of South Western Pipe Line."

"What deputy took the call at the Pipe Line Company?"

"I gave the call to SO7, Charlie Parker," replied the dispatcher. "Should I call him?"

"Have him give me a call on the landline," Craig said.

Craig continued writing down the things he felt were major elements in the search. He noted that Brown was possibly driving a white Lincoln Continental. He is probably in possession of firearms.

The U-Haul trailer is important. He'll probably ditch it before he'll ditch the car. The phone ringing interrupted his thoughts. When he answered, it was Charlie Parker on the line.

"Hi ya, Charlie," Craig said. "How goes it?"

"My butt's dragging, Sheriff," was the response.

"I hear ya, Charley, but tell me, what was taken from the Pipe Company?"

"Someone went into the trailer that they use as an office and ate food that was in the fridge and walked off with a pair of boots and a set of coveralls."

Hearing what Charlie had to say made Craig more certain that Brown had been the one out on Highway 91.

"Make sure that Kevin Marcy gets a copy of your report," Craig directed. "Thanks, Charley. Be talking to ya."

After hanging up with Charlie, Craig continued to list the things that he knew and what he wanted the public to know about. He had taken a map of the county from his desk and, with a red grease pencil, drawn a line from a short distance south of Rock Springs to I-80. He then extended the line along the line on the map showing I-80 to Point of Rocks. The only way Brown could have gone from there would have been east on I-80 to Wamsutter or to Exit 187, which was the Baggs Road at Crescent Junction. After Baggs, he'd end up in either Craig or Granger, Colorado.

Craig picked up the phone again and dialed the number for the Sweetwater County Road and Bridge Department and asked for his friend Ted Hicks. Craig explained what was going on and asked Ted to have his crews keep an eye out for the U-Haul trailer and the Lincoln, and Craig put all of the pertinent information in the form of a news release and had his administrative clerk distribute it to the media sources.

Since the SO had requested an armed guard, Fred Dreskel had responded himself. He was dressed in the CPI uniform with eagles on the shirt collars. A holstered Smith & Wesson .357 Magnum hung from his utility belt.

There were twelve beds in the ICU with blue curtains providing separation. There was the sound of machines breathing and IV units beeping. Several nurses busied themselves, checking equipment and monitoring vital signs.

Steve Lolly was standing by and was sitting at the nurses' station. The station was situated in the middle of the unit. When he saw Fred, he had gotten up and walked with him through the entrance and closed the door behind them.

"Wow!" Steve exclaimed. "We got the boss on this one."

"Sherrie said she needed the best we had," Fred replied through a big grin.

Steve gave Fred a rundown on events from the escape to the finding of Cappers as he knew them. "The guy that thought he'd killed Cappers is still out there," Steve was saying. "When he finds out that he's still alive, things could get nasty around here."

"Is hospital security clued in on this?"

"No. We want as few people as possible to know who we're guarding," Steve cautioned. "If anybody asks, we're guarding a jail inmate that had a fight."

"Okay," Fred acknowledged. "I'll post myself right outside this door so that I'll be able to head off any trouble before it gets inside. It'll be Amy and me pulling twelve-hour shifts for the next couple of days, and then I'll integrate some other people."

"How do you communicate with the sheriff's office?" Steve asked.

"I have your frequency in my company radios," Fred replied.

"Good deal. If this guy comes around, call me," Steve said as he was walking down the hall toward the exit.

CHAPTER 10

"The young man had been beaten and suffered severe injuries to the head and neck. According to a sheriff's office spokesperson, it is suspected that the escaped prisoner being sought may be involved. He is now armed and considered extremely dangerous," the radio announcer was saying as Brown awakened.

He had pulled off the black-topped road last night and driven down a dirt road to find a place to hide the car and trailer before daylight came. The road had ended at a tank and an oil derrick that was not pumping. He had turned out the car lights and sat still for a while. The moon was still out, so it didn't take long for his eyes to adjust.

He could see that the road ran through a canyon with rocky walls on each side. *Perfect,* he had thought to himself, *now I need to dump this trailer.* When he had gotten out of the car to stretch his legs, his feet made crunching sounds on the light covering of frozen snow that covered the area. The sound was so loud, it caused him to stop and look around.

He had unhooked the U-Haul from the car's hitch and moved the car so that it was heading back up the road. He still had plenty of gas, so he had kept the car running, the heater going, and the radio on while he stretched out on the front seat for some rest.

"Damn!" he had said out loud. *I wish I had heard the rest of that radio broadcast;* he thought as he had rolled down the window on the driver's side of the car. He hadn't opened the window before he had fallen asleep, and all the windows were fogged up.

Stuck above the car visor was a map that he hadn't noticed before. He traced his finger along I-80 until it came to the intersection of I-80 and Baggs Road. He remembered the sign where he had turned off the interstate. He couldn't find the dirt road on the map, but he knew he couldn't be more than a few miles from Baggs Road.

"They know I'm armed," he said aloud to himself. *I should of put a bullet in that guy's head. If they know I've got a gun,* he thought. *They know that I've got the car, and they'll be looking for it. I can dump the trailer, but the car is got to get me out of here.* He'd have to wait till dark and find another car somewhere. This one would be too easy to spot.

Clouds had begun to build in the sky and daylight was waning when Brown had decided to get out of the canyon. He didn't know much about weather, but those clouds looked scary. He needed out before snow or rain began to fall.

Leaving the canyon, he came upon Baggs Road. Just as a few small ice pellets began to fall. He had decided to head south and hoped that there was enough gas to reach Baggs. The gas gauge showed less than a quarter of a tank.

It wasn't long before he came upon a road sign that read "State Line Road 43." Just below that, it read "Baggs 24." It was dark now, and the ice pellets had turned to snow, and he had to use low beams in order to see. After about thirty minutes, the snow stopped, and Brown could see lights ahead. There weren't many. He began to wonder just how big Baggs was. As he had gotten closer, he noticed that most of the lights were on houses on the right side of the highway. There were very few on the other side.

There was what appeared to be a little store and gas station on the right side of the road in what could have been the middle of the town. Brown noticed several pickup trucks parked there. Each of them had their engines running, and the steam was coming out of the exhausts. He drove the car into the parking lot and behind the store. Lights were turned on in one of the pickups, and it pulled away and headed south.

Brown turned the engine off, took the map, and stuck it in the pocket with the gun. He sat for a few moments before getting out of the car, then walked around to the front of the building. The glass in the door and one window was frosted over. *If he can't see in, they can't see out,* he thought. Moving quickly, Brown quietly opened the door of a pickup that had its engine running. It was an automatic, and he quietly put it in drive and allowed the truck to roll forward and guided it onto the highway. He then turned on its lights, closed the door, and sped down the highway.

Craig, Martha, and Katie sat around the table after dinner, discussing the treatment options that were available for Martha's type of cancer. For over an hour, Martha described, for Katie's sake, how Craig's mother had suffered as she struggled with the effects of chemo. She spoke about the nausea and the occasions when she would throw up and how her body would convulse with dry heaves. She told of the lack of energy and how Mrs. Spence often couldn't drag herself out of bed. Martha remembered that just when Craig's mom was beginning to feel like a human being, it was time for her to be taken for another treatment, and it would start all over again.

Craig had heard Martha describe his mother's battle before, but this was the first time Katie had heard the story. In fact, this was the first time she had realized what the ramifications of cancer treatment could be.

"Is it possible that there have been improvements in the treatment?" Katie asked.

"Sure there has," Martha explained. "I understand that there have been improvements in the chemical recipes used in chemo, and dosages can be measured better."

"Also, a combination of chemo and radiation can be used according to the doctor," Craig chimed in. "I'm told that some people aren't bothered by the chemo as much as others."

"That's right," Martha agreed. "I have a friend that lost her hair, had a little nausea after each treatment, and lost some weight but didn't have a terrible time at all."

"What do you think you wanna do, Mom?" Katie asked.

"I think I want to have a double mastectomy, do the chemo, and follow it up with radiation treatments."

There was silence for a long moment. Katie and Craig looked at each other, and then Katie found her voice, took her mother's hand, and almost with disbelief asked, "Isn't that a little radical, Mom?"

"That's exactly what it's called—a radical mastectomy."

As Craig and Katie continued to try and grasp what Martha had decided, she went on, "I remember that your mother went through all of the breast treatment, and on a follow-up exam, they discovered that while the spots had disappeared in her breast, the cancer had moved into the lymph nodes, and they decided to do surgery. She didn't last long after that. We've caught it early. There's no indication that it has gone anywhere, but the breast. Let's get rid of the breast before the cancer moves on."

"It's your call, doll," Craig conceded. "If that's your decision, let's go for it."

"Mom, when did you decide?" Katie asked.

"Just now," Martha responded. "I got to thinking. I'm not going to have any more children. I'm too old to be concerned about making men's eyes pop out, and they're just a load to carry around. Why take a chance on the cancer moving or coming back? Let's hit it where it lives."

CHAPTER 11

Craig had spent most of the morning in court. The ACLU was pursuing their suit to force the county to close the jail. The attorneys had just argued back and forth and made motions, and the judge kept denying them. Finally, the judge had had enough, and he carried the hearing over for two weeks.

Back in his office, he was anxious to see what progress was being made tracking down Brown. His desk spindle had several notes stuck on it, and he began pulling them off one by one. The first one was from the Green River Sentinel. He put it aside and took off the next. It was from the Catron County Sheriff's Office. He put that one next to the phone. He'd call soon. He checked the other messages. There was a message from Martha. He had barely picked up the phone when the dispatcher's voice came over the intercom.

"Sheriff? You there?" she asked.

"I'm here. Whatcha need?"

"I've got the Catron County Sheriff's Office on the line. I'll patch it through."

Craig put the message to call Martha in his shirt pocket as his phone had begun to ring.

"Craig Spence," he said into the receiver.

"Hey, Sheriff Spence, this is Deputy Hopkins up in Rawlins." There was a short pause, and Hopkins continued, "We found that white Lincoln you been looking for."

"Ya don't say," Craig said, not trying to hide the excitement in his voice. "Where'd ya find it?"

"Over in Baggs. Your guy dumped it and stole a pickup."

"What about the U-Haul?" Craig had asked.

"No, no sign of it," Hopkins replied.

"He must have ditched it somewhere between the interstate and Baggs," Craig surmised. "Could ya make a sweep of that area and see if he ditched it on a side road?"

"Sure, Sheriff. You gonna send somebody to pick up the car?"

"Yeah, I'll have it picked up and brought back here," Craig assured him. "Thank ya for the help."

"Anytime, Sheriff, see ya," Hopkins said before hanging up.

In very short order, Craig had dispatched his detectives to Catron County along with a flatbed vehicle transporter. He spent the next hour on the phone with the offices of his counterparts in Colorado, where Brown would have to pass through if he went south out of Baggs. Craig, Colorado, would be the next town of any size, and he might just need to get something to eat or at least buy something for the road.

Craig had spread a large topographical map on his office floor and was on his knees examining every section between Wamsutter, Wyoming, and Craig, Colorado, when Steve Lolly walked in.

"You looking for anything special, boss?" he asked.

"I'm really uptight about that U-Haul. If Brown tied that woman up and left her in that trailer, she's going to freeze to death, if she hasn't already." There was a long pause, and Steve got down on one knee beside Craig.

"Look here," Craig said, using his right index finger to draw an imaginary circle on the map. "He ditched that trailer somewhere in this area. "There are several little roads that run off the main road, but they don't go far. They go to oilrigs, pumping stations, or storage tanks."

"One thing we know for sure," Steve said. "He didn't go cross-country with that car." Using his finger to point to a road on the map, Steve continued, "Look at this one, boss. It goes off the main road, goes out into the prairie a mile or so, does a horseshoe, and comes right back to the main road. There' a name for it there. Cowboy Road it's called."

Craig got up and went to his desk. He pushed the button that would connect him to the dispatcher.

"Get a hold of Hopkins over in Catron County and patch him through," Craig instructed.

"You think you're on to something, boss?" Steve asked.

"My gut says that trailer is on Cowboy Road. According to the map, there's a pumping station that sits back there between two ridges. A perfect place to hide something for a while."

"I've got Hopkins on, Sheriff," Dispatch said. "Go ahead."

"Say, Hopkins, Spence here."

"Yeah, Sheriff, this is Hopkins."

"What's your 20?" Craig asked.

"Halfway between Wamsutter and Baggs Road," came the reply.

"Got a map of Catron County handy?" There was a long pause after Craig's question.

"Had to pull over, Sheriff. Got a map. Whatcha got?" Hopkins wanted to know.

"There's a side road about ten miles south on Baggs Road called Cowboy Road. Sound familiar?"

"Yeah, it's a road used to service a pump out there. You think maybe?"

"Just a hunch, but we really need to find that trailer in a hurry. That missing woman might still be in it," Craig said, indicating some urgency.

"Let's hope not," Hopkins said. "It's well below freezing out there."

"With any luck, he's still got her with him, but we can't count on it," Craig warned.

"Take me about thirty minutes to get there. I'll get back with ya pretty soon. Out." The patch was broken.

"What's new with the guy in ICU?" Craig asked Steve.

"If infection doesn't set in, he has a good chance of healing up. He's going to be a sore puppy for a long time."

While waiting to hear from Hopkins, Craig settled back in his executive chair and listened while Steve brought him up to date on the investigation.

After talking with Stacey Cappers and getting security set up, Steve had driven five miles south on Highway 91, turned around, and slowly drove north, inspecting the right shoulder. He had driven approximately three miles when he spotted what appeared to be a box of some type. It turned out to be a plastic toolbox. Close by was a large flat-bladed screwdriver with blood on it. There were also marks on the ground that looked as if something had been dragged for several yards. Steve had collected the box and the screwdriver and took photos of the area. When he returned to town, the evidence was sent to the crime lab in Cheyenne for processing, and a technician in the photo lab downstairs was developing the film from his camera.

Forty-five minutes after Craig had relayed the information about Cowboy Road, the dispatcher patched through a call from Hopkins.

"That gut of yours is working overtime, Sheriff," he said. "I'm parked about fifty feet from a medium-sized U-Haul. It's been here a while because the tracks have been filled in by a light dusting of snow, and there hasn't been any snow fall since early last night."

Craig and Steve both were sitting forward on their chairs in anticipation of what else Hopkins was going to say.

"As soon as I get some pictures of the trailer and the area, I'll see if I can open it," Hoskins continued. "I yelled a couple of times and turned on my siren, but there is no sound coming out of it."

"10-4," responded Craig. "I'll stand by."

The minutes that they waited seemed like hours. Steve sat on the edge of Craig's desk, fidgeting with pencils that were stuck in a coffee mug. Craig leaned back in his chair; his cowboy hat pulled forward on his head so that his eyes were just visible below the brim. His hands were folded across his stomach, and he rotated the thumbs around each other. Suddenly, Craig leaned forward and pushed the button for the dispatcher.

"Dispatch," he said. "When Hopkins comes back on, give him our secure frequency. I'll be tuning in to it."

"What are you thinking, boss?" Steve asked.

"There are tons of people monitoring police frequencies. We might not want this for all to hear."

"Boy, I'm glad you thought of that," Steve said. "The last thing we need is the media getting a hold of stuff before we even know what we've got."

Craig and Steve continued to wait. Craig opened his lower right-hand desk drawer and took out a half pint of Johnny Red and two shot glasses. He poured until each glass was half full and shoved one over to Steve before putting the bottle back in the drawer. Craig downed his, feeling the familiar burning on the back of his throat and down to his stomach.

"Sheriff Spence, Hopkins here," the voice came through the speaker.

"Spence here, go ahead."

"I got the U-Haul opened. The woman is there all right. Looks like she's been dead for a while. I'll get the state boys notified and keep this place guarded until they get on it."

"Would you take enough pictures of the trailer and the surrounding area that we can have a set?" Craig asked.

"I'll take a couple of rolls and have our tech make plenty of prints. I'll fax you a copy of my report, Sheriff," Hopkins said.

Craig stood, stuck his hands into the two hip pockets of his trousers, and walked slowly around the room. Neither he nor Steve spoke for a few minutes, and then Steve broke the silence.

"I'll get out an update on that APB, boss. This guy is now wanted for two murders and an aggravated assault," Steve said as he slid off the desk and started for the dispatch area. Hearing a desk drawer being opened, Steve glanced over his shoulder and saw Craig place a holstered Smith & Wesson chief on top of the desk and take a box of ammo from the drawer. As he watched, Craig loosened his belt and slid it through the belt loop on the holster. The last time Steve had seen Craig wear a weapon was when he went after an oil field worker that had kidnapped and killed a twelve-year-old girl. As Craig was buckling his belt and adjusting his sidearm, Steve walked out of the room, remembering what went down the last time Craig put on a gun.

CHAPTER 12

The gas and oil boom had just begun in Wyoming, and wells were being drilled in much of Sweetwater County. There was a cluster of wells being drilled just outside of Bairoil, a town up in the northeast part of Sweetwater County. Only 179 people had inhabited the town before the drilling and pipelines being laid. Like most towns in southwest Wyoming, the influx of humanity was overwhelming, and the pressure on the limited young female population should have been expected.

Craig only had a part-time deputy in Bairoil. When the distraught mother called in about her daughter being missing, the deputy, who also owned the local grocery, was busy taking inventory, preparing for his next trip to Rawlins for supplies.

Between sobs, it was determined that a twelve-year-old girl had been missing for two days. She was last seen with one of the roustabouts that had just moved into town and was staying in his camper just outside of town. When the deputy and several of the town's residents went looking, the camper was gone.

Craig had taken two deputies with him to Bairoil, and when he got there, the townspeople were gathered at the store. Everyone there had a rifle or a handgun. The part-time deputy had his hands full, trying to keep the group calm.

When Craig got out of his car, the crowd surrounded him, and everybody was shouting at once, and he couldn't understand anything being said. He pushed his cowboy hat to the back of his head and put both hands in the air, palms forward, and the crowd began to be quieted.

"I'm glad you're all here, so I don't have to round you up!" Craig shouted above the low murmuring that was still going on.

"We're going to kill that son of a bitch when we catch him!" someone shouted from the crowd.

"We've got a little girl to find," Craig said. He didn't have to vshout now. The crowd was quiet. "By the way," he continued, "if there's any killing to be done around here, I'll be doing it." Craig paused a moment, surveying the crowd, then he asked, "Is that clear?"

When he was sure he had everybody's attention, Craig began to get things organized.

"If there are any landowners here, I want you to go to your place and search every inch of it. All of you have CBs, so if you find anything, call in on the store's CB. We'll set up the command post here. You guys head out."

Craig waited and watched as a few people in the crowd moved away to waiting pickup trucks, and then he began again.

"Let me see a show of hands from those people that have horses," he asked. Several in the group raised their hands.

"We've got three hours of daylight. Get your horses and ride the sage outside of town and any arroyos in the area. Ride in groups of twos. If you find anything, one of you ride back here." A few more people left the group. Most of those left were women and a few teenagers.

"The rest of you, go down to where that guy had his camper parked." Craig pointed in the direction he wanted them to go. "Spread out on both sides of the road and walk that area going away from town. We'll walk as much as we can before dark. If you find anything, somebody come running."

After everyone was off on their way, Craig had let out a sigh of relief. He wanted everybody busy while he and his deputies did their jobs. The roustabout they were looking for had an account at the store. His name was Norman Gaither. Craig got his name, a description of his truck, and the name of the company he worked for. The company had offices up the street. He and one of the deputies called on the oil company and found out at which rig their suspect was working. Before

Craig could head out to the rig, one of the searchers on horseback came galloping up to the store.

"We found the girl," he said.

"Where is she?" Craig asked.

"Down in the arroyo that runs through my forty acres over to the north. She's been shot twice in the chest."

Craig sent his deputies along with the rider to secure the scene while he notified the state criminal division. When he had gotten off the phone, he turned to the Bairoil Deputy.

"You got an extra gun?" he asked.

"Yeah, Sheriff, got a .38 Ruger under the counter."

"Get it for me," Craig had said through clenched teeth. "I'll need your car."

For what he needed to do, Craig didn't want to use a marked squad or in any way telegraph who he was when he got to the rig.

It was about a thirty-minute trip across some pretty rough country on a rutty dirt road. There were several pickups and oil service vehicles parked alongside the road. Sure enough, there was the truck that had been described to him. The drilling was in full operations, and there were about ten or twelve people on and around the rig. Craig pulled the car alongside one of the service trucks and decided to wait until Norman went for his truck. He knew that the rig would go on all night, but the crew would change.

On a rack across the truck's back window, Norman had two rifles. One of them was a 30-30. The other appeared to be a .22 long rifle. Craig checked the position of the .38 revolver stuck in his belt at the small of his back. He made sure that he could come up with it if he had to. Craig had waited close to an hour when several pickups pulled up and parked. He knew the crew was about to change. He started the car and sat with it idling. If he needed it, he didn't want to take a chance of it not starting.

A tall man went for the truck. Craig sized him up to be about 6'4" and 250 pounds. He had a beard and wore a fur-covered hat with the flaps pulled down over his ears. He was carrying a plastic cooler. As the big man reached for the driver's door; Craig leaned through the car's window and called out.

"Norman Gaither?"

"Who wants to know?" the man had asked, continuing to open the truck's door.

"Sheriff Spence. Need to talk to ya," Craig said as he got out of the car and strolled toward the truck, holding up his cased badge in his left hand. Craig stopped a few feet from the truck, keeping an eye on every move the truck's occupant made. The man rolled down his window and pulled the truck closer to Craig, and Craig asked again, "Norman Gaither?"

The cooler the guy had been carrying caught Craig right across the nose, and it knocked him off his feet. The truck sped out across the field and got back on the road, heading to the main highway. With blood dripping from his nose, Craig got the car onto the road and gave chase. On the front passenger's seat was a red light that was plugged into the cigarette lighter. He put it up on the dash and flipped the switch as he tried to make up the distance between them.

After a couple of miles, they ran into the portion of the road that had deep ruts, and the truck ahead of him began to jump and buck, finally spinning out and flipping on its side, the side and rear windows popping out. Craig came to a stop and hurried toward the truck. He remembered the rifles in the rack. Just as he got to the truck, Norman was climbing through the window. Craig grabbed him by the collar of his jacket and pulled. The big guy came out right on top of him.

When Craig rolled free and got to his feet, the guy was crouched, holding a utility knife, the kind most men in the oil fields carry.

"I guess I don't have to ask you about the girl now, do I?" Craig said as he backed up a little, putting some space between them.

"Didn't want to hurt her, but she kept screaming. I swear I didn't want to hurt her," Norman said as he now had begun to move in a circle around Craig.

"Why didn't you just let her go?" Craig asked, keeping Norman in front of him.

"She was going to tell her dad what we'd done, and she kept screaming it."

"We can talk about this without anybody gettin' hurt. Put the knife down."

"Not you, not nobody's taking me." Norman lunged for Craig, thrusting the knife at his midsection. Craig sidestepped and caught the side of Norman's head with a left hook, sending him down to a knee, but he was right back on his feet and circling again. When he got near the truck Norman bolted to it, reached through the broken back window, and grabbed the 30-30 off the rack.

There was a sharp crack. A cauliflower blossom appeared on Norman's jacket where the insulation was pouching out. Norman stumbled and began to level the rifle again when the second shot entered his chest just below the other.

When the medical examiner arrived to remove the body, it appeared that Norman had just sat down. He was leaning a little forward with one leg doubled under him, just sitting there with a surprised expression fixed on his pale dead face.

CHAPTER 13

The hospital was a hive of activity when Craig got there the next morning. Nurses in their starched white uniforms were darting in and out of doors with signs over them that read radiology, outpatient surgery, pediatrics, and physical therapy. People hurrying along the halls to keep appointments were maneuvering around patients in their hospital gowns, trying to keep their backsides covered with one hand and pushing their IV stands with the other.

Craig could see the sign at the end of the long hallway that read "INTENSIVE CARE UNIT" in big bold letters. That's where he was going. Telling Stacey Cappers his mom was dead was his job. The closer he got to the intensive care unit, the more distasteful the task became. Just inside the unit door sat Amy Dreskel, behind a small table where she recorded information on everyone that visited the unit and whom they came to see. She looked good in her uniforms, Craig thought to himself. Her brown shirt with silver leafs on the collar and the badge that rode on the top of the left breast really looked sharp.

"Hi ya, doll," Craig greeted her.

"Sheriff, it's good to see you," Amy said as she stood and gave Craig a hug. "What brings you out so early?"

"I need to talk with Stacey," Craig said almost in a whisper. "How's he doing?"

"They've got him sedated pretty good, so he sleeps a lot," Amy replied.

"Has he said anything to you about what happened to him?"

"Not a thing. When he's awake, he just asks if I know where his mother is."

Craig pushed his hat back on his head and let out a deep sigh. He looked straight into Amy's eyes and shook his head.

"Maybe we should let the nurse know before you tell him," Amy suggested. Craig nodded his approval, and Amy went to the nurses' station and came back with the charge nurse. She was a tiny lady with short dark hair streaked with gray, like most women who have been in the nursing field for a long time.

"You needed to talk to me, Sheriff?" she said with a smile.

"Yes, ma'am," Craig said respectfully. "I've got some bad news for Mr. Cappers, and I wanted to check with you before I tell him."

"What kind of news is it?"

Craig leaned down close to her ear before whispering what he had come to say.

"His mother is dead," he said.

"Oh my," the little nurse gasped as she placed her hand alongside her face. "I think I'll need to clear this with the doctor. In fact, he may want to be here when you tell him."

Craig watched as the nurse hurried to the nurses' station. Looking around, he could see people in beds with equipment attached and tubes running in all directions. He noticed that the place was cold and wondered how these people could stand it. Then the nurse came back.

"The doctor doesn't think he'll grasp what you tell him because of the medication he's on. However, he's given me instructions as to what to do if things don't go well."

She beckoned for Craig to follow her, and she led him around a room partition to a bed at the far end of the room. Stacey was lying on his right side, and his left arm and shoulder was bandaged and tapped to his chest. An oxygen tube was in his nose, and an IV was in his right arm. One side of his face was obscured by dressing covering the wound on his head. The nurse spoke softly to him, "Mr. Cappers, are you awake, Mr. Cappers?"

The eyelid of the eye not covered by bandages fluttered and slowly began to focus. He turned his head just slightly so that he could see who was in the room. The part of his face that was exposed was purple, black, and blue from bruising.

"Mr. Cappers," the nurse continued. "Sheriff Spence would like to talk with you. Do you understand what I'm saying?"

"Yeah," the voice was raspy and weak.

"Would you like for me to raise your bed up a little and make you more comfortable?"

"That would be nice," Stacey responded. "Could you put a pillow behind my head too?"

The nurse adjusted the bed and stuffed a pillow behind Stacey's head. He appeared to be comfortable and awake now. She nodded to Craig, and he reached out to take Stacey's good hand.

"Hi ya, Stacey," he said. "They tell me you're gonna make it."

"Yeah, that's what they say," Stacey said matter-of-factly. "What can you tell me about my mother?"

"She tried to protect you, Stacey." Craig paused and looked into that eye staring at him, waiting for him to go on. "She didn't make it, son."

The eye closed and the lips pursed so tightly that the area around them was white. A lone tear built up in the corner of the eye and began the journey across the bruised cheek and into the ear. Stacey began to shake, and Craig took his hand in his as the sobbing began. The nurse brought a plastic cup of water and gave Stacey a pill. He was reluctant at first, but after some sympathetic urging by the nurse, he released Craig's hand, took the pill, and drank the water.

"Is there anyone I can call for you?" Craig asked.

Stacey reached out and removed a tissue from a bedside table and wiped the tear from his ear and blew his nose before answering.

"We lost Dad a couple of months ago," Stacey started but paused to blow his nose, and between sobs, he continued, "I was taking her to Gillett, Wyoming, where I'm working. There's no one else."

Craig spent over an hour at Stacey's bedside and listened. Stacey told him about his being an only child and how his mom and dad had brought him up in Arizona and the plans that his mom and he had made now that his father was gone.

"Where is my mom?" he had asked finally.

"We'll take care of her until you're up and around," Craig replied. "We'll need you to give us a positive ID when you can. By the way, have you remembered anything else that you didn't tell my people before?"

"No, Sheriff. Wish I could remember something that would help you catch the bastard." The soft sobs began again.

It was a little before noon when Craig left the hospital and he had made a stop at the medical examiner's office, where he learned that Mrs. Cappers had died of strangulation. Now he needed to follow up with Catron County, but he'd decided to go home and have lunch with Martha first.

"Hey, doll, what's for lunch," Craig called out as he closed the door behind him.

"You should have told me you would be home for lunch," came a stern reply from someplace in the far corners of the house.

"I needed a calm, friendly atmosphere to relax in," Craig countered with some sarcasm. "Guess I overestimated the tranquility of home."

Martha came into the living room from the direction of their bedroom with her hands on her hips.

"You underestimated my tendency to be annoyed when you just bounce in and announce that you're here for lunch."

"Might I be forgiven?" Craig took Martha's hand and led the way to the kitchen. Craig sat her down at the table, and he proceeded to make ham, lettuce, and tomato sandwiches. They sat across from each other and indulged in light conversation for a while when Martha brought him back to reality.

"Have you told that young man about his mother yet?"

"I was at the hospital earlier and I told him." Craig paused for a moment. "There's no one else in that family. His dad's gone, and he was taking his mom to Gillette, where he could take care of her."

"Poor thing," Martha said sympathetically. "Is he going to be all right?"

"With any luck and if infection don't set in, he'll be fine physically," Craig replied.

"What's the latest on that inmate's whereabouts?" Martha inquired.

"We don't know where he is, but the whole western U.S. is keeping an eye out."

"I worry," Martha said quietly. "He's got nothing to lose now, and someone else is sure to get hurt."

"Yeah, doll. That's my gut feeling too," Craig said as he rubbed his hands across his face and ruffled the thinning hair on his head. "He's got a stolen truck, and it's too cold for him to just ditch it. He'll get rid of it, but he'll have to steal another, and that'll lay out a trail."

"I'm glad he's out of this county," Martha said as she had begun to clean the table. "Don't want any of our boys getting hurt."

Craig got up and gave Martha a squeeze.

"Gotta go, doll," he said.

"Thanks for lunch," Martha replied. "I'm not annoyed anymore." They both laughed with each other as she walked with Craig to the door.

The wind had come up again, and Craig had to hold his hat with one hand while he pulled the door shut with the other. He glanced up at the sky and saw that the sky was clearing, and rays of sunshine were beaming through the breaks in the clouds. *It's gonna be a cold night if those clouds blow away,* he thought as he crossed the street heading for his office.

The spindle on his desk had several notes on it. The top one was a message from a reporter from the *Rocky Mountain News.* He put it aside. There was nothing he wanted to say to the press right now. He'd just wait; they'll call back. The next one was a call from the state crime lab in Cheyenne. He dialed the number on the paper. A nondescript monotone voice answered the phone.

"Criminal Investigations Department, Crime Lab. How can I help you?"

"Hi ya, Sheriff Spence, Sweetwater County returning your call," Craig said into the phone.

"Ah yeah, Sheriff, we processed some evidence for you on the Cappers case." The voice began to take on a little life now. "My chief told me I should give you a holler as soon as I had something."

"Great, whatcha got?" Craig asked.

"We were able to raise several fingerprints off the toolbox. We got a match on your victim.

There was also some blood splattered on the toolbox consistent with the blood found on the blade of the screwdriver. It came from the same person."

Craig listened intently while the voice paused. Then it began again.

"We managed to get a thumbprint off the screwdriver's handle that didn't belong to your victim. It matches the prints you sent us on your escaped prisoner, Albert Brown."

"I had a hunch that he was involved in this," Craig said.

"That stuff you sent us will be brought down by currier tomorrow, Sheriff."

"Thanks," Craig responded. "You guys do a great job. Be talking to ya."

Craig leaned back into his chair and closed his eyes. He tried to imagine what Brown would do, where he'd go. *No doubt he knows we know he has a stolen truck. If I were him, I'd stay away from towns until after dark. He's got another problem, though. He's going to run out of gas. It's either steal another vehicle or buy gas and take a chance that someone recognizes the truck.*

Suddenly, Craig sat up in his chair. He had just thought of something that had rung a bell in his head. Those guys, Brown and Watson, had come to town on a Greyhound bus. They had probably traveled all over the country on buses. He would feel comfortable on a bus.

Craig grabbed the phone book from his desk drawer and turned the yellow pages to "bus" and found the number to the Greyhound bus station in Rock Springs. When he got the agent on the line, he asked for a schedule and a list of Greyhound bus stations in Wyoming and Colorado to be faxed to his office. The agent was very cooperative and agreed.

Craig pushed the button on the phone that would connect him to the chief deputy's office.

"Yeah, boss, this is Steve."

"Get up here and bring Kevin with you, I've just had a brain thrust," Craig said excitedly.

Steve and Kevin had come into the office together, and each sat in one of Craig's plush lounge chairs. Kevin looked as though he hadn't slept for days. He had bags under his eyes, and he needed a shave.

Steve, on the other hand, was as spite and shined as always. The creases in his uniform shirt sleeves looked as though they would cut if they were touched. The brass on his collar reflected the light from the ceiling, and his cowboy boots were spit shined.

"You look terrible," Craig began with Kevin. "What's going on?"

"I've been working with Catron County, trying to clean up the crime scene, running evidence and blood samples to the lab, and visiting with Cappers periodically to see if he remembered anything."

"When we get through here, go get cleaned up and get some sleep," Craig directed. On his desk, Craig spread out the schedules and station locations that the Greyhound Station agent had faxed to him and motioned for Steve and Kevin to come over to his desk.

"Brown and Watson had traveled all over the county on a bus," he began. "I'm willing to bet that Brown is going to board a bus when he ditches that truck he stole."

"Does anyone know how much gas was in the truck he stole?" Steve was looking at the list of bus stations in Wyoming as he asked.

"According to the owner, he'd just filled it up in preparation for a long day in the oil fields the next day," Kevin said. "That means he had a full tank, which could last him three to four hours."

"Yeah," Craig said. "You need to remember that he's going to hole up somewhere, and he'll use a lot of the gas staying warm. I don't think he's gone too far, but I think we'd be smart to have the county sheriffs check around their towns where buses stop and see if they can spot that truck."

"Okay, boss," Steve said. "I'll also let the highway patrol in on it too. They hang out around most towns."

"While you do that, I'm going to take the sheriff's advice," Kevin announced. "See you in a few hours unless you get something."

It was Tuesday afternoon, three and a half days after Albert Brown had successfully made his escape from the Rock Springs City jail, that the first positive break came. Craig got a call from the chief of police in the town of Hanna, a small mining town just off I-80, in the eastern part of the state, just west of Laramie, Wyoming. Craig knew the chief, Norm Francis, because he had been a patrol commander on the Rock Springs Police Department for a time. When his attempts to be selected to the chief's position at Rock Springs weren't successful, he applied and was accepted as police chief in Hanna. Craig never cared much for Norm. Craig felt that he was a braggart and was too quick to use excessive force. *He also spent too much time chasing prostitutes,* Craig thought.

"Say, Spence, Chief Francis here," Norm had said over the phone. "What's this you let some killer get away?"

"Some of us ain't perfect Norm," Craig had replied. "What can I do for you?"

"Uh, uh," Norm started. "It's what I've done for you."

Craig was beginning to get irritated, but he kept his temper in check.

"I really got things to do, Norm," Craig had said. "If there's something you need to say, spit it out."

"You been looking for a truck, Spence?"

"As a matter of fact, I have," Craig said. "Why?"

"Was this truck reported stolen out of Baggs a couple of days ago?"

Craig sat up straight in his chair and took his hat off and placed it on the desk.

"What are you trying to tell me, Norm?"

"I found the truck." Norm paused before going on. He was listening to hear the effect of what he'd said. "I just had it towed to our impound lot. You want us to process it, or you want to do it yourself?"

"We'll get to the truck later, just hang on to it," Craig said as he stood up. "Does the Greyhound bus stop in Hanna?" Craig asked.

"It does now, but since the mine shut down, they're talking about cutting it out. You plan to take the bus up here?"

"Never mind, what time does the bus stop there?"

"Depends on which way you're going. If you're going to Cheyenne, it comes in around eleven in the morning. If you're going to Salt Lake, it stops about two fifteen in the afternoon."

Craig looked at his watch: it was 3:45 PM. If Brown took the bus east, he was long gone, but if he took the one to Salt Lake, he's only been on the road for a little over an hour.

"How long you think that truck has been where you found it?" Craig asked.

"Wasn't there this morning around six because we worked a rollover on that road until about ten."

"Can you find out how many people boarded the bus to Cheyenne this morning?" Craig asked.

"If you think your guy might've gotten on that bus, your luck is holding out. That bus broke down just before it got to Elk Mountain and never made it here."

"How about the one this afternoon?"

"I'll call you back in a bit." There was a dial tone, so Norm had hung up his phone.

Craig began to pace as he waited for Norm to call him back. After a few moments, he sat at his desk and took out his map. Using the straight edge of a sheet of paper, he measured the distance from Hanna to Rawlins to Rock Springs. He calculated that the distance was about 150 miles. The bus could cover that in a little over two hours. The schedule showed that the bus made a stop in Rawlins for thirty minutes, so it was there now. The ringing of the phone broke his concentration.

"Spence here," he said into the phone.

"It's Norm," responded the voice on the other end. "One guy and two women got on the 2:15. The guy was wearing a blue down jacket, jeans, and a Cardinals baseball cap. The bus left at 2:40 . . ."

CHAPTER 14

It was pitch black on either side of the highway. The truck's headlights lit the road ahead and reflected off the frosted grasses just off the shoulders. Brown kept glancing in the rearview mirror, but beyond the glow of the truck's taillights, there was only darkness. Occasionally, off in the distance, there would be a single light that must have been at a pumping station or a storage tank, he thought.

After what seemed to have been hours, there was a road sign. "Dixon, 10 miles," it read. As he drove through the night, he had passed through several little towns. Some with strange names, such as Savery and Encampment. When he passed through Saratoga, there was no activity on the street, and he had wondered to himself what it would be like to be able to live in a nice small quiet town.

Albert Brown's mom had moved to Baltimore from Ocean City, Maryland, when the city got tough on the prostitution trade, and she could no longer supplement her waitresses pay. Albert and she lived in a nice apartment just off the main strip. The location had been perfect for Albert and his friends who were all in their teens. They would raid the shops and sell the shoplifted merchandise to the tourists. If they got spotted by the shop owners, it was easy to get lost among the tourist on the crowded streets and make their way to Albert's house until the cops, who were too busy chasing prostitutes and busting johns to waste much time chasing a group of kids who were ripping off a few shops.

So Albert lived on the southeast side of Baltimore, Maryland, in the projects, not far from the waterfront. There were eight buildings in the complex, each four stories high and the upper floors accessible by stairs or elevators that always smelled like piss. He and his friends made sure that the lightbulbs in the stairways were always out, and they'd stop the elevators on the second or third floors so that people would have to take the stairs.

There was a fence in balcony on each floor, so they'd have a lookout in front of the building; and if an elderly person entered the building, the lookout would give a signal, and the person would be accosted in the stairwell, robbed of their money, groceries, or whatever they had that was worth taking. Security guards were finally put to patrolling the projects, and Brown and his friends had to find other places that were easy pickings.

Albert's mom worked at a bar down on the wharf, so he and his friends began to hang out on the waterfront, rolling drunks and stealing change off the tables. Everything was fine until one merchant marine they tried to roll wasn't as drunk as they thought, and he put one of Albert's friends in a choke hold. Albert struck the guy over the head with a wine bottle, and there was blood squirting everywhere. Albert never stopped running until he got to the Greyhound bus station, and he never looked back. When he got to Barstow, California, he called his mom and she moved west.

Another road sign had come in to view. "Walcott and I-80, 6 miles," the sign read. He had pulled to the side of the road and checked the map when he realized that he had driven almost in a circle and was now about to cross I-80 again. He'd have to get rid of this truck, he thought. The gas gauge was just a little below a quarter, and in the distance, he could see that the sky was beginning to turn a grayish color. Day would be breaking soon, and he'd need to ditch the truck before sunup.

After Walcott, he had continued on Highway 287/30 and reached the town of Hanna when he saw flashing red lights ahead. *This is where we part company,* he said to himself as he pulled the truck into a dry creek bed off the side of the road. Leaving the truck, Brown walked into town, past a sheriff's cruiser and a tow truck that was trying to upright a pickup. No one paid any attention to him, and he walked until he came upon what appeared to be a coffee shop or a restaurant. There was a small sign in the window that said, "BUS STOP." Brown decided that no matter where this bus was going, he was going to be on it.

"Thanks, Norm. Are you at the bus stop now?" Craig asked.

"No, but I have the agent on another line."

Craig had taken a moment to think and look at the map before answering.

"Norm," he began. "Have the agent get in touch with that driver. Have him take his time as he heads for Rock Springs. Tell him to come up with an excuse to stop at the Bitter Creek rest stop." Craig flipped a switch on his communications system that would allow him to override all other units.

"This is Sherriff Spence. All units go to frequency number 2," he said. Frequency number 2 was the department's secure frequency.

"All units, head to Bitter Creek rest stop. Stop short of the rest stop for further instructions, 10-4?" (understood?)

One after another patrol units and detectives on duty acknowledged receipt of the transmission.

"SO2 and SO3, my office now. All units return to normal operating frequency," Craig directed.

Within minutes, Steve and Kevin were standing in front of Craig's desk. Neither had a clue as to what was up, but they didn't remember a time when the sheriff had acted with such urgency.

"There's a bus that should have left Rawlins a little bit ago," Craig began. "Our guy Brown is likely on it."

Steve and Kevin pulled chairs up to the desk and sat leaning forward attentively as Craig brought them up to date. The ringing phone interrupted Craig.

"Spence here. Yeah, Norm, what's up? Oh boy, we're finally getting a break," Craig said excitedly. "Thanks, Norm."

Craig hung up the phone and checked his watch before relaying the news to Steve and Kevin.

"That bus is still in Rawlins. It had to wait for a connecting bus from the town of Lander that got delayed by road conditions," Craig said with a smile on his face and then began to lay out his plan.

"I don't have any idea how many people are on that bus, but I've suggested that the driver make up an excuse to stop at Bitter Creek," Craig explained. "I want to set up around the rest stop before the bus gets there. If we're lucky, most, if not all of the passengers, will get off to stretch their legs, including Brown. We'll want to isolate him from the rest of the group. I have no reason to believe he'll give up without a fight." Craig stopped talking and waited for some input from Steve or Kevin.

"There are always several 18 wheelers parked in there," Kevin began. "If we can alert them so that they will be ready to seal off the area we can just sit and wait him out if we have too."

"Okay, that's your assignment," Craig said. "He's believed to be wearing a blue down jacket, jeans and a Cardinals baseball cap."

"Steve," Craig continued, "I want you to get your best shooter out there and position him so that he'll be able to take Brown out if it comes to that."

"Not a him, boss," Steve said with a big grin on his face. "She's off duty, but I'll get her headed that way, and I'll position the patrol units so that we can block him in case he decides to rabbit."

"Let's head out," Craig said as he stood and pulled his cowboy hat securely on his head.

There were a lot of empty seats on the bus. It had pulled out of Rawlins late, but only a couple of people got on from the bus they had been waiting on. Brown had curled up in two empty seats with his head against the window and the top of the backseat. The cool glass felt really good. It wasn't long after the bus pulled out of Rawlins that he'd found himself nodding off and waking when his head would fall away from the backseat.

Brown was startled by something striking the side of the bus. He sat up and looked out the window. There was a big truck passing, and it was throwing slush against the bus. He had also noticed that the truck was moving faster than the bus. He thought it odd that the bus was moving so slow. Leaning forward and peering between the backseats in front of him, he had been able to see through the bus's windshield and the lane the bus was in was pretty dry. There was slushy snow piled up between the lanes. He had also seen the driver's face in the rearview mirror. Brown had watched him for a long minute then turned back to the window. *Why did the driver keep glancing in the rearview mirror?* he asked himself.

All the traffic going in the same direction as the bus was passing and throwing slush against the buses side. Brown peered over the top of the seats in front of him and locked eyes with the driver who was looking at him in the rearview mirror. His curiosity got the better of him, and he moved up the aisle and knelt on the floor where he could talk to the driver.

"Ya wanna trade places and let me drive? Brown asked. "Hell, what's with this thing?"

"Got power loss," the driver responded. "There should be another bus waiting for us up the road another forty-five minutes."

"You mean we creep along like this for another forty-five minutes?"

"Afraid so," the driver responded.

Brown had glanced at the speed odometer that was registering a little over forty-five miles an hour. He looked down at the driver's foot and noticed that there was a lot of room between his foot and the floor.

"You shouldn't be out of your seat like this, sir. I must ask that you return to your seat," the driver had spoken with a hint of sternness in his voice.

"Do me a favor," Brown had asked as he stood up and was holding on to the partition between the driver and the first row of seats. "Push that pedal to the floor."

"Sir, please take a seat."

"Damn it, push the damn thing or I will." The irritation was building up in Brown's voice.

Before the driver could react, Brown stomped on his foot, and the bus lurched forward for a second, throwing Brown off balance and into the aisle on his back. When he got up, he reached inside his jacket and pulled the gun.

"I don't know what you think you're pulling, but it smells fishy as hell. You get this thing rolling at seventy-five miles an hour, or you'll end up walking," Brown warned.

A woman passenger began to emit little, short screams.

"Oh! Oh! Oh god! Oh please! He's going to kill us! Oh! Oh! God!" she shouted.

"Shut your mouth, lady!" Brown yelled at her and pointed the gun at her face. "Now get out of that seat and find another one. You in the other seats too, find another seat. Move it."

The people occupying the seats three rows deep had all moved toward the back of the bus. Brown could hear whimpering and some crying. Somebody was praying out loud. Some people were peering over the tops of the seats in front of them. Others had leaned out in the aisle just enough to see what was going on. Brown stood with one foot in the stairwell of the bus and faced the rear. He yelled out, "Everybody, just stay in your seats! Nobody gets hurt unless you get stupid." Turning to the driver, Brown demanded to know what was going on. The driver had been hesitant. "Look, ya dumb bastard, you tell me what's goin' on, or I start shootin' up this bus."

"They're waiting for us," the driver said.

"Who?"

"The cops."

"Where?"

"Next rest stop."

"How far is that?" Brown asked.

"About another forty miles," was the driver's reply.

Brown reached over the driver's left shoulder and ripped the radio phone off its mount and beat it against a rail until it fell in several pieces. He could see a small town coming up ahead, and the driver identified it as being Wamsutter. He needed to get rid of most of these people. Watching them and keeping the bus driver from being a hero was more than he wanted to deal with. *The longer I let them have to make plans, the more apt they are to make a move on me,* he thought.

After passing through the town of Wamsutter, he made the driver pull to the side of the road and stop the bus.

"Okay, everybody out," he said. "Don't make me tell you again." The seats behind the driver were a perfect place for him to stand so that he would be out of the way and still watch everyone exiting the bus. When the woman that was screaming earlier tried to get off, he grabbed her and sat her in the seat next to him.

"You might come in handy," he said to her.

She begged him to let her get off, but he stuck the gun against the back of her neck and whispered close to her ear.

"Somebody's gonna die today. You want it to be you?"

"No! Please don't hurt me," she begged him.

"Then shut up and sit still," Brown demanded. "What's your name anyway?" he asked.

"Gladys," she answered through whimpers.

She was a tiny thing, and she was so afraid that her body was trembling as she sat next to this maniac with a gun. Her hair was chopped just below the ears, and she wore a part in the middle. She held the collar of her red jacket tight around her neck as if to shield herself from what was happening. Why didn't he let her off with the rest of the passengers? She had asked herself. *What's he going to do to me? Will I ever see my mother again?*

Gladys was from a small town by the name of Rye. The town was snuggled against the front range of the Rocky Mountains a few miles south of Pueblo, Colorado. Homes were mostly of the log cabin variety. The main street was unpaved, and anyway, townsfolk liked it just like it was. Artists, writers, photographers, and tourists frequented Rye because of its peacefulness and scenic beauty.

Gladys's family owned a curio shop just off the main street, and Gladys spent most of her time out of school and, in the summers, helping about the store. Now after winning an art scholarship, she was on her way to the University of Utah to begin her freshman year.

"Oh god, help me!" She didn't mean to shout out loud.

"Gladys," he almost shouted her name, "if you don't stop that whining—" Brown stopped in midsentence.

The road sign coming up caught his eye. "Table Rock, next right," it said, and up ahead he could see the turnoff, and there was a motor home parked on the ramp. He got an idea.

"Take the next turnoff," he said to the driver, who at once began to slow the bus down.

"Pull up behind that motor home and stop."

The motor home was a sleek rig with alternating shades of brown strips that ran the length of the body and around the back. It was the type that the sides telescoped out to form an extra room. There was a bicycle and a motorbike stowed on a rake on back. After the bus had come to a stop, Brown got the attention of both Gladys and the driver.

"Listen up," he said. "I want both of you to get off the bus and walk ahead of me to the door of that thing. I have nothing to lose, so don't be dumb. When we get to the door, Gladys, you knock on it. Let's go."

The driver opened the door, and all three stepped off the bus and walked toward the front of the motor home. Gladys knocked on the door like she had been told. An elderly man appeared at the door and peered through the window. After giving the three of them a quick looking over, he must have pushed a button because the door opened, and he stepped down on the ground.

"Can I help you folks?" he asked.

Without a word, Brown shot the old man right in the face. For a moment, he just stood there. Blood spurted from a hole just below where the left eye had been. The blood had splattered on everybody. Then like a slow-motion movie, he had collapsed, lying on his back with blood still spurting like a fountain from that hole.

Gladys fell to her knees. Her hands, with the fingers spread open, were over her eyes. Her mouth was open and squeaky, screeching sounds escaped. Some of the blood had splattered on her hands and had begun to run into the sleeve of her jacket.

Gladys's whimpering had really begun to unnerve Brown. Grabbing the back of her jacket with his free hand, he had propelled her through the open door of the motor home.

"Get in there and shut up," he told her.

Turning to the driver who was on his knees bending over the old man, Brown yelled, "Drag him over to the bus and put him in the baggage compartment, and hurry."

After the body had been dragged feet first to the bus and stowed, Brown ordered the driver into the motor home along with Gladys.

"What the hell is your name anyway?" Brown asked.

"Ed," came a timid reply.

"Well, Ed, look in the storage compartments under the seats and find some rope."

Brown began opening cabinets while Ed raised the cushions on the benchlike seats. Brown found a roll of duct tape.

"Here," he called out to Ed. "take this and tie her up, hands and feet."

While Ed went about doing as he was told, Brown had become interested in what appeared to be some type of radio receiver on the console. Keeping a close eye on Ed and the gun pointed in Ed's direction, he watched little lights blink in sequence across the face of the receiver. Every time someone transmitted, the light stopped, and only the light tuned to the transmitter stayed on. When the transmission stopped, the light sequence started again.

"What the hell is that thing?" he asked Ed, who had finished binding the hands and feet of Gladys and was sitting beside her.

"It's a scanner," Ed had advised. "You can hear people talking on radios. When going cross-country, you can hear road and emergency crews."

"How about police?" Brown asked.

"Probably."

Brown watched the little lights and heard several transmissions that sounded like road crews joshing with one another. Realizing he had wasted enough time, he turned to Ed and held the gun at arm's length, pointing at Ed's head.

"I should do you right now, but I want them cops to know I outsmarted them."

"Why don't you just let us go and go on about your business?" Ed asked.

"My luck's run out. I've spent my whole life in one jail or another. After this trip, they'll never quit. I'm a dead man walking as they say. It's a game now, so here's what you do."

Brown paused a moment to listen to a conversation over the scanner. A Wyoming highway patrolman was calling for a tow truck at mile marker six on Black Butte Road. Brown gave Ed his orders.

"You go back to your bus. She goes with me." He swung the gun and pointed it at Gladys and then continued. "You wait ten minutes after I'm gone before you even start the bus. If I look in the mirror and see that bus, she's dead."

Gladys let out a woeful moan and rolled on her side, so she could look at Brown.

"Please, you don't need me, let me go with Ed," she pleaded tearfully.

"Oh yeah," Brown had said through a knowing grin. "You and me gonna get tight."

He motioned to Ed to get out, and as Ed got up to leave, he patted Gladys on the head and hurried out the door. Once Ed had cleared the door, Brown closed it, climbed into the cushy captain's chair behind the steering wheel, and pushed the button marked "Engine Start." He could hardly hear the engine when it started, but the instruments on the console danced, and the vehicle responded to his pushing on the gas pedal.

Craig had positioned his people so that they would have the bus surrounded once it pulled into the rest stop. The patrol cars were hidden behind the restrooms, and a sharp shooter was on top of the building using the air conditioning unit as cover. There was a lobby in the building, and women's restroom was at one end and the men's at the other. Craig and Steve had positioned themselves in the foyer while Kevin was in one of two big rigs he positioned to block off the entrances and exits once the bus was inside. Steve made sure that the cars that did pull in parked away from the entrance to the toilets.

As Craig looked around, he knew this was the ideal place to have to do this. There was lots of open space and good cover provided by the picnic shelters. As far as the eye could see, in either direction, there was nothing but open range. The Wind River Mountain Range was barely visible on the horizon to the north, and the terrain was pretty barren to the south.

Craig noticed that the wind was picking up. Loose snow that had lain out in the prairie was being blown across the highway and across the parking area of the rest stop. Rivulets of white blown snow chased one another across the highway, around the concrete trash receptacles that lined the parking islands and out into the sagebrush, dancing and curling their way over open range. The conditions were right for a ground blizzard that would make for poor visibility.

"Hey, Sheriff," the officer on top of the building called out. "The bus is coming."

Craig stepped out so that he could see down the highway. He could see a good five miles of straight highway. The bus was coming.

"Everybody heads up!" he'd shouted into the wind.

Everyone had hunkered down behind whatever obstacle was available—a picnic shelter, dumpsters, parked eighteen-wheelers, and the restroom building. Craig took one last look around before positioning himself inside the building. He left the door cracked so he could see the bus. There it was, pulling into the parking lot. Craig saw the eighteen-wheeler pull across the entrance so the bus couldn't go out the way it had come in.

The bus pulled into the slots where tractors and trailers and RVs park. Before it had come to a complete stop, Craig's men were positioned on both sides of the door, crouched low with guns drawn while waiting.

The door of the bus opened, and the driver stepped out. His face was pale, and there was blood on his white shirt. He sat down on the ground with his head in his hands.

"Who's on the bus?" an officer asked.

"Nobody," came the reply.

Officers stormed the bus to see for themselves. Confirming that no one else was on the bus, they stood by as Craig came up and sat down beside the driver.

"Hi ya, ole buddy," Craig said as he approached. "You look like ya been wrung out pretty good. Where're your passengers?"

"Wamsutter."

"How come?"

"The guy got suspicious and pulled a gun. Made everybody get off except me and a woman," the driver related as he lit a cigarette that one of the officers had offered. He was still shaking from what he'd gone through and what he'd seen. He told Craig how he had been made to stop at Table Rock and how the old man in the motor home had been shot.

"So where did the guy with the gun go?" Craig asked.

"He found some tape in the motor home. Made me tie up the woman. Told me to get back in the bus and wait ten minutes. He said if he looked in the rearview mirror and saw the bus, he'd kill the girl. After seeing what he did to the old man, I believed him. So he drove off and I waited."

"Whatcha do with the body?" Craig had inquired while motioning to his crew to gather around.

"He's in the luggage compartment."

"Tell me about the hostage," Craig asked. "Had she been hurt in anyway?"

"She's probably in her middle twenties. She's scared to death. Spent most of the trip crying and whining. At one point, the crazy guy got pissed off at her, but he didn't hurt her."

Craig understood that time was not on his side. He began to give direction to the people gathered around him. He directed Kevin to have someone take the driver and process the scene where the killing had occurred. Steve was to contact the highway patrol, give them a description of the motor home, and have them shut down the interstate, westbound, at the Rock Springs Airport exit.

"Be sure you let them know that Brown is driving the unit and he's armed. Add that he has a hostage and has nothing to lose," Craig directed. The rest of the officers were directed to go ahead to the roadblock and close in on the vehicle from behind. Craig had the driver open the luggage compartments on the bus and directed the deputy to take the driver's statement as soon as he could. Craig knew that if the statement wasn't taken pretty quick, much would be forgotten, or there would be time for the story to be embellished.

A plastic bag was stuck to the head by the coagulated blood. With his utility knife, Craig cut the bag away from the flesh, being careful not to further damage the remains. The head looked like a watermelon that had been hit with a hammer. The bullet appeared to have entered just to the left of the left nostril, taking out the cheekbone and left eye.

Craig unzipped the bloody jacket and found papers folded and stuck in the inside pocket. A manufacturer's certificate of origin, transfer documents from a dealer in Florida to a dealer in Salt Lake City, Utah, and a letter authorizing Donald Burch to ferry a 1981 country coach model motor home.

In the right hip pocket of the deceased man's trousers, Craig found a wallet containing a driver's license issued to Donald Burch, whose date of birth was August 6, 1939, and address was 2030 Sestren Avenue in Tampa, Florida. Kevin, who had been taking pictures of the bus and evidence being collected, took charge of the papers, and he and Craig agreed that it was time to call the coroner.

There was only one patrol deputy left in the parking lot. Steve had marshaled everyone else and was leading a convoy west on I-80.

The Wyoming Highway Patrol had been alerted, and a statewide alert had been instituted. A roadblock had been set up at the exit to the Sweetwater County Airport by the highway patrol, and the Rock Springs Police Department was blocking all exits to the city. What none of the law enforcement agencies was aware of was that there was a scanner in the motor home, and Brown was monitoring all radio transmissions.

The scene on the off-ramp at Table Rock didn't appear to have been disturbed. Not much traffic at this time of day. As Kevin took pictures and looked for any evidence that could be collected, especially the cartridge casing, Craig had walked across the highway to a gas station that was near the eastbound on-ramp. He learned from Peggy, the lady running the place, that the driver of the motor home had come over to use the phone to call someone to fix a carbon monoxide leak. He had told her that he was getting a headache, and the alarm had gone off.

"Why didn't he park the motor home over here someplace?" Craig asked.

"I just don't have the room for such a big rig. No one else would be able to get in here," was the answer he got.

"Did you see any activity over there where the motor home was parked?"

"A bus pulled up behind it, but I thought they were just checking on his welfare," replied the station manager.

"How about people?" Craig continued to inquire. "Did you see any of the people that were on the bus?"

"I could only see the tops of them rigs over the crest in the road. I didn't see nobody."

"Did you hear anything after the bus got there?"

"With the trucks and cars going by plus the wind, I wouldn't have heard nothing."

The station manager told Craig that after the man got off the phone, he stayed around for a little over an hour and a half, waiting for help to arrive from Rawlins. During the wait, he had told her that he owned a small company that ferried vehicles across country and that he was supposed to drop the motor home off in Salt Lake City. He hadn't been gone more than fifteen minutes when the bus pulled up. She told Craig that she still hadn't seen anything that looked like a maintenance truck.

Brown was listening to the cops talking to one another, chatting about what they were doing and what the motor home looked like and that there was a hostage on board and that everyone was to hold their fire. Two tractor trailers had been commandeered and used to block the highway with just enough space between them for other trucks and cars to maneuver between them. Brown heard them say that when the motor home was spotted, the two trucks were to be backed against each other.

Gladys, tied up and propped up on the bench seat, could hear Brown giggling every time he heard somebody talking. Her wrists were hurting, and she had to go pee. It was obvious that this guy was out of his mind and could care less about what was going to happen.

"Hey, you!" she called out. "I gotta go pee."

"So what are ya tellin' me for?" Brown yelled back over his shoulder. "There's a toilet on this thing someplace. Go find it."

"I can't walk with my feet tied like this," she reminded him.

Brown broke out in a giggling fit and looked at her in the mirror.

"Guess you gonna have to piss your pants, huh?" He continued to giggle. "Tell you what, you roll yourself up here, lie on your stomach, and stick your feet in the air. I'll try to take the tape off."

Rolling herself off the bench onto the floor and scooting up to the captain's chair actually took some of the pressure off her bladder. It seemed to take him forever to rip away the tape, and the urge was back. Finally, her feet were free, and she had gotten to her knees and was able to stand. She still was going to have fun trying to get her clothes out of the way with her hands tied, she thought.

"How about my hands?" She thought she'd try.

"You can piss all over yourself for all I care, not happening."

While she was on the toilet the motor home made a violent swerve. Not able to catch herself, she had fallen off the stool. As she sat there on the floor, the humiliation of her predicament and the fear of what was ahead started the tears flowing. Crawling out on her knees, she could see through the motor home's windshield that they had left the interstate. They were on a two-lane blacktop, and there was a sign that read, "Superior 12 miles."

The scanner had gone quiet. Brown was watching her through the rearview mirror trying to pull her underclothes up over her butt with her hands tied behind her. He was amused and whistled at the sight of her upper thighs and bare behind as she struggled to get her panties up. The humiliation of what she must look like with her pants down around her knees turned the silent tears into audible sobs.

The afternoon daylight was waning fast under cloudy skies. The hilly snow-covered terrain did not provide any access where he could get off and hide the motor home. According to the dash clock, it was four o'clock, and it was going to be dark soon.

Craig and Kevin were headed back toward the rest stop when Steve called on the radio.

"SO1, SO2."

"Go, 2, SO1 here."

"One, that motor home never reached the roadblock, and we're backtracking to see if it's stopped on the highway," Steve advised.

"Send a patrol car up the superior road and up the road leading to Sweetwater Coal," Craig directed. He thought for a moment, then continued, "If it's spotted go slow and just observe, remember there's a hostage."

"10-4, boss."

Craig remembered something the station manager had said. There was a carbon monoxide problem. With the temperature falling as it gets later, he'll have to keep it going to keep warm. He let Kevin in on what he was thinking.

"That station manager told me that the reason Mr. Burch had stopped was because of carbon monoxide setting the alarm off and giving him a headache. I'm betting that Brown ain't moxy enough about one of those rigs to know that he can run the heater off a generator, and he'll keep the engine running wherever he holds up."

"Maybe, but then we lose the girl too," Kevin observed.

"Not necessarily," Craig surmised. "She is probably scared silly. I don't know, but maybe that highly stressful state will help her stay awake, and she'll get sick to her stomach but won't pass out.

"I don't think stress will save her at all," Kevin disagreed. "I don't care about him, but I'd hate to lose her that way."

Their conversation was interrupted by the radio. It was dispatch advising that the town marshal at Superior was on the phone, and he had spotted the motor home. It was parked in a crevasse in the cliffs were the main road dead-ends. It was backed in, so anybody approaching could be seen.

Craig knew the area, and he could picture the cliffs in his mind. He knew exactly where the break in the cliff wall was that a motor home could be parked. Brown was trapped. The only way out was the way he went in.

"By gosh, I've got an idea," he said to Kevin as he took the mic off its clip and pushed the transmit button. "SO2, SO1," he said.

"SO1, this is SO2. Be advised that Ed, the bus driver, has informed us that there is a scanner on board the motor home."

"Dad gum it!" Craig exclaimed. "SO2, meet me at the store at Point of Rocks."

That asshole has been monitoring everything we've said, no wonder he left the highway, Kevin mused.

At the store, Kevin pulled up alongside Steve's car so that he and Steve were directly across from each other. Craig had gotten out and walked between the cars so that he could see the faces of both men. When he spoke, there was excitement in his voice.

"We're going to have to move fast, but carefully," Craig had begun. "Steve, you don't know this, but we've found out that there is a carbon monoxide leak aboard the motor home. That can work in our favor or if we miscalculate, we lose the hostage. I know the area where that motor home is parked, and we can get to it without being seen."

Both Steve and Kevin had listened intently, neither wanting to interrupt because Craig seemed to be on to something.

"Steve," Craig continued. "You take a couple of cars and set up just outside of town in case something goes wrong, and he tries to rabbit," he said. "Kevin, you and I are going to take a dirt road that starts at the power plant and goes across county to the top of those cliffs just east of Superior. We will be on top of the cliffs looking down on the motor home. He'll either recognize the monoxide problem and come outside, or he'll pass out, and we will be able to break in and take him without a fight."

"What about the girl?" Steve had asked.

"You find a phone and contact the town marshal," Craig had directed. "Tell him to alert the fire department to stand by for a call from us. You'd better alert the ambulance crew at the power plant too. Keep your fingers crossed. Let's go do it."

CHAPTER 15

Martha had nervously kept herself busy for the last couple of days: waxing floors, washing drapes, going through picture albums, and remembering. She was reading some old letters that Craig had sent from Korea when the phone rang. It was the call she'd been waiting for but dreaded a little. It was the scheduling office at the hospital in Salt Lake.

After saying who she was and satisfying herself that she was talking to Martha Spence, the scheduling tech told Martha that the oncologist wished her to meet with the surgical staff on Monday of next week. The meeting was set for 8:00 AM in the same location where she visited with the oncologist.

When she hung up the phone, Martha just sat on the floor beside the phone stand and allowed her mind to ask the questions that she had tried to avoid ever since the diagnosis. *Should I have gotten a second opinion?* she asked herself. *How am I going to feel with no breast? What will it feel like while it's healing? Will I want to have reconstructive surgery? What will Craig think of me? What will I look like after surgery? Will I need more surgery? Is this surgery right for me?*

Her thoughts were disrupted by Katie calling from the back of the house. She had returned from shopping for this evening's supper.

"Mom! Where are you? I'm back."

"I can hear that," Martha called out as she got to her feet. "Sure are noisy."

"Were you sleep or something?" Katie asked.

"No, I was trying to think," Martha replied sarcastically. "What did you want?"

"Just wanted to let you know I was home. Boy, are we grumpy today."

Martha had begun to pick things out of the bags that Katie sat on the kitchen table: carrots, frozen corn, sweet potatoes, pork chops, and a container of her favorite ice cream, chocolate ripple.

"Got a call from the hospital," she said.

"What did they say, Mom?"

"They want me there on Monday to meet with the surgeon."

"That's great that they aren't wasting any time, don't you think?"

"I guess," Martha was wistful.

"Are you having second thoughts, Mom?" There was concern in Katie's voice. "What's wrong?"

"Nothing's wrong, I've just been thinking things that I hadn't wanted to think about before, like what I'll look like when it's over, or what Craig will think, or should I see somebody else, things like that."

"Have you said anything to Dad?"

"No, silly, I just started thinking these things after I got the call, and you're not going to say anything either," Martha said while shaking her fist playfully at Katie.

"I'm going to call the office, see when Dad will be home, so I'll know when to start supper," Katie said as she dialed the number to the sheriff's office. Martha began to put the groceries away and was putting the ice cream in the freezer when Katie yelled out to her.

"They've got Brown cornered!" she called out. "They're out in Superior. The whole department is out there together with Dad."

"This could be a long night. I don't think he'll make it for an early supper. My gut tells me that this guy is not going back to jail," Martha commented as she sat at the table. A worried look came upon her face. "Your dad is getting too old for this crap."

"My wrists are killing me, and I need to get out of this jacket. I'm so hot I feel like I'm going to throw up," Gladys was saying as Brown tried to find the switch that would turn the interior lights on.

"Yeah, I hear ya," Brown said as he was getting out of the driver's chair. He glanced out of the side window into the night. There were other campers parked around the area. Some had generators going that provided them with lights. The low steady humming of the generators could be heard inside the closed motor home.

It was getting stuffy, Brown noticed. The heater was really putting out. The dash lights were still on, and the gas gauge showed a little over half a tank of gas left. *Maybe enough to get through the night,* he thought.

"Hey, man, please," Gladys pleaded.

Brown stowed the gun in his jeans at the small of his back and moved over to Gladys. She was whimpering again. She'd been tied up a long time.

"What will you do for me if I untie you?" Brown asked.

"I won't make any trouble for you," she said. "I promise to stay out of your way."

"I can't believe you're really that dumb," Brown said as he rolled her over so that her arms that were taped behind her back were easy to get at. He felt along the taped wrist until he found the end of the tape. Gladys heard the tape being unstuck from itself, but then he stopped pulling. "What's wrong?" she asked.

"I think everything is going to be just fine."

She could almost hear the smirk on his face. Brown put his hand under her jacket and down the inside of her pants. She stiffened as he placed his hand over the left cheek of her butt.

"No! No! No!" she cried out as she kicked and squirmed to dislodge his hand. She had never been able to secure her pants after going to the bathroom, and he easily pulled them down below her knees, making it difficult for her to direct her kicks at him. She was now in complete hysterics, and she began to scream and call for help. Brown grabbed her legs and put them over his shoulder, locking them there with his left arm and pushing forward to prevent her from kicking. He placed his right hand over her mouth to muffle the screams and bent her legs so far toward her head that his mouth was only inches from her ear when he spoke.

"Listen, broad. You make another sound and you're a dead piece of meat. I'm going to get some of your ass if I have to kill you to do it."

He slowly took his hand from over her mouth. There was no screaming now, just sobs and coughing. With his free hand, Brown began to remove her panties. He had gotten them up her thighs when she began to puke and gag. Almost simultaneously, there was a shrill pulsating noise coming from the middle of the motor home.

Startled, he rolled free of Gladys onto the floor. When he jumped up, he experienced dizziness, and he was light headed. Feeling his way along the walls, he got to the alarm and ripped it from its mounting and stomped on it until the sound stopped. He began to feel like his stomach was upset. He thought that fresh air might help. He opened the door of the coach and stepped outside.

When Brown had pushed her legs up toward her head, Gladys had managed to slip her arms over her butt and was able to place her hands over her exposed private parts. After he left her, she continued to work her legs through her arms until they were now in front of her. Brown had left a piece of tape sticking out from the wrapped wrists, and she hurriedly took it in her mouth and began to strip the rest of the tape. Between bouts of retching and gagging, she finally got the tape off.

She hadn't eaten for a while, so there wasn't a lot that she threw up, but what was there was all over her jacket and the seat. The odor was putrid, and she fought to get her hands to work so she could be free of the jacket and get herself covered with her clothes.

Kevin slowly inched the patrol car across the desert on a rutty dirt road. It was dark, and as they saw the glow from the town's lights, Craig had instructed him to only use the parking lights. The road dropped down off a mesa and cut between two huge rock formations. Craig had Kevin stop the car. They both got out, and Craig came around to Kevin's side. Craig whispered to Kevin, "You stay here while I try and spot the motor coach."

Kevin nodded, indicating that he understood, and Craig moved away, feeling his way along the base of the rocks until he was able to look over the town on the left and the right. They had said that the motor home was in an opening in the rocks. Craig remembered an opening where teenagers used to have keggers, smoke pot, and play loud music on their pickup stereos. It would be on the left, about a hundred yards or so farther down. He went back to where Kevin was waiting.

"That opening is about a hundred yards down," Craig said to Kevin.

"Yeah, I know," Kevin replied. "We used to party out here when I was growing up."

"Good, because we need to find a way that we can come in behind it. There's enough glare from the town's lights and the other campers that we will be seen coming up in front."

"There's a dirt bike trail that goes up to the top at the back of that opening," Kevin remembered. "We can go up on top and come down it, and no one will know we're there until we want 'em to."

Craig thought that was a great idea. He and Kevin walked back up to the mesa and down the ridge until they came to the bike trail. The coach was there in the opening just like they said. They could see a dim light through a side window. Against the glare of town's lights, a plume of steam was visible in the air behind the coach.

"The engine on that thing is still running," Kevin thought out loud.

"Which means that whatever lets the carbon monoxide in hasn't done it yet," Craig surmised. "Let's move on down the hill and get closer."

They'd only walked a short way down the trail when Craig stopped abruptly and stuck out his arm, signaling Kevin to stop. They stood frozen in place for what seemed to Kevin to be a long time.

"What'd you see?" Kevin asked.

"Nothing," Craig replied. "I thought I heard a woman screaming."

"If you did, maybe we're too late for the girl," Kevin said.

"Hell, I hope not—" Craig stopped in midsentence. "Hear that?" he asked.

"Sounds like some kind of alarm, don't it, Sheriff?"

"I think that's our cue to move in. You take the left side and position yourself in front. I'll take the right side. If he's not unconscious, he'll be coming out."

"You want him alive?" Kevin asked.

"We'll take what he gives us," Craig replied.

It was cold outside the motor home, but the cool, fresh air made Brown feel much better. His stomach wasn't as queasy as it had been in the coach. He took some deep breaths and was watching the steam from the warm air that was expelled when he heard the door of the motor home slam shut. Rage welled up inside of him, his throat tightened, and he made growling sounds as he pulled out the gun and began pounding on the door.

"You little bitch, I'm gonna kill your ass. Open the door!" he yelled, all the while thinking to himself that he should have killed her long ago.

Using the wrap around bumper as a step, he hoisted himself up high enough to grasp the rearview mirror. He could now see inside through the window in the door. Gladys had opened a sliding window on the opposite side and had her head stuck through it.

"Help me! Somebody please help me!" she screamed.

Brown, really pissed off now, jumped to the ground and started around the front of the coach, running headlong into Kevin, who was working his way from the other corner. Two shots in quick succession shattered the quiet.

Craig heard the shots. One was the pop of a small caliber and the other was the kaboom of Kevin's .357 revolver. As he approached the main door of the coach, he heard Kevin yell.

"I'm hit. Comin' your way!"

In the dark, Craig could see a person stumbling, moving in a wide arch around the front of the coach where he was standing.

"Police, give it up!" Craig shouted as he leveled his .38 Smith & Wesson snub-nosed chief.

The person kept coming, gradually moving more in the direction of the coach in hesitant, jerky movements, as if the person wanted to focus but couldn't tell where Craig's voice was coming from.

"Give it up, Brown, your last chance!" Craig shouted again.

People were coming out of their campers that were parked nearby, and Craig could hear Kevin yelling to them that they were police and to stay inside. Then there was a bright reddish-yellow flash over the top of Craig's outstretched hands, and the little chief was bucking— once, then twice.

The crash with Kevin had caused Brown to discharge the Glock 9 prematurely. The bullet entered Kevin's upper left thigh, and he later learned that it had just missed the femoral artery and had passed through, causing very little tissue damage. Had that artery been severed, he would have bled out before emergency crews could have gotten to him.

Realizing that Brown was heading straight toward the sheriff, Kevin crawled up to the right front wheel of the coach. The pain was excruciating. He could see Brown moving through the darkness, but he couldn't see the sheriff. He saw the flash from Brown's gun and heard the sheriff return fire two times . . .

"All units, shots fired. Officer and suspect down. 10-20 against the cliffs east side of town," Kevin said over his radio. "You okay, Sheriff?" Kevin called out.

"Yeah, you?" came the reply.

"Hurts like hell, but I'll live. Got me in the leg."

Gladys heard the shots out front, and she watched through the windshield as Brown staggered toward the rear of the coach. She had no idea there was someone else out there until the shooting started again, and then she saw all the flashing red and blue lights coming toward her. There was somebody knocking on the door.

"You all right in there, darlin'?"

It was a man's voice, but all she could see was a cowboy hat through the window in the door. The whole area was ablaze with pulsating lights, and people were rushing around. She watched as a group of people was working on Brown. Some were tending to his right foot while others were working in his chest area. There was another group in front of the motor home working on somebody. There was more knocking on the door.

"You can open the door now, doll. It's all over."

The door opened, and Gladys stood for a moment, staring down at this man in a cowboy hat, looking up at her with a big smile on his face. He stuck out both arms.

"Come here, little lady. You don't know how glad I am to see you," Craig said to her.

She stepped down into his arms and knocked his hat off as she threw both arms around his neck and hugged him tightly.

"Thank you, thank you, thank you," she said over and over as she clung to him as if her life depended on it.

"It's gonna be okay," Craig said as he carried her to one of the ambulances that had responded.

"Wrap her up and check her out, will ya," he said to a young lady in a paramedic uniform.

"You betcha, Sheriff," she replied. "Come sit with me," she said to Gladys as she led her to the back of the vehicle.

The bullet from Kevin's gun had torn through Brown's right boot and pretty much blew out his ankle. Both rounds from Craig's gun had found their mark. One entered the stomach just below the navel; one entered his rib cage on the right side and came out up in the chest, just above the sternum. Craig watched the paramedics work on Brown, and he couldn't help but think that by the grace of God, that's wasn't him.

On his way over to check on Kevin, he walked by where a deputy was digging at a hole in the side of the motor home. Remembering about where he was standing, the bullet Brown fired at him missed by about two inches. Craig pushed his hat to the back of his head and spoke to the deputy.

"Sure glad you're digging that bullet out of there instead of me, ole buddy."

They had placed Kevin on a board and were carrying him past Craig to an ambulance.

"How you doing?" Craig asked.

"They say I'll be fine. It went clear through."

"Is there anything you need me to do for you?"

"Yeah, Sheriff. Can I have a couple days off?" They both laughed out loud as Kevin was placed on a gurney and shoved through the doors.

There were two ambulances at the scene: one from the fire station in Superior and the other from Sweetwater Power Plant. They both pulled out at the same time headed for Rock Springs and the hospital. One was carrying Kevin and Gladys and the other carrying Brown. Craig stood and watched the lights weave their way through town and out onto the main road.

"Need a ride home, boss?" It was Steve. "I've got the state boys coming, and we'll be working here all night. Why don't you go home?"

"I'll just take Kevin's car when I'm ready to leave," Craig answered. "Did you arrange for security at the hospital?"

"All taken care of. CPI will meet the ambulance, stand by till he comes out of surgery, and then stay with him in ICU, assuming he makes it."

"Here," Craig said as he unbuckled his belt, slid off his holstered snub nose, and handed it to Steve, "just in case the boys from the state want it."

It was after midnight when Craig finally pulled on to I-80 and headed toward Rock Springs. He pulled in behind a tractor and trailer rig that was one of several snaking their way through the night, the running lights reflecting off the ice crystals that floated through the cold air.

Craig found himself reliving the events of the day: the story surrounding the senseless death told by the bus driver and the hostage. *Boy, she must have been scared,* Craig thought to himself. *If we hadn't gotten there when we did, she'd probably be dead, or worse.* He wanted to hear her story too, but it could wait. He'd read the detective's report in the morning.

Steve getting hurt weighted on Craig's mind some. He began second-guessing the way the situation was approached. *Was there something we should've done different?* he asked himself as he watched the headlights reflect off patches of highway ice. *Sure am lucky,* he thought, slowing the cruiser a bit. *That bullet, had it been down a bit and to the right, I'd be on a slab right now.* The radio disrupted his thoughts.

"SO1, Dispatch," the voice shattered the quiet.

"Go ahead, Dispatch," Craig answered.

"SO1, they need you to stop by the hospital on your way in."

"10-4, Dispatch, what's up?"

"SO1, they want you to sign some custodial documents. Brown didn't make it out of surgery."

Craig didn't answer right away. Instead, he pulled the cruiser to the side of the road and just sat for a moment.

"SO1, Dispatch, do you read?"

"Dispatch, SO1, have Sherrie call off the security detail," Craig directed.

During the drive to the hospital, Craig thought back over the years and the few times that he had taken a man down. There had always been a certain amount of remorse or regret. Not so this time. A feeling of relief and satisfaction settled over him. Some people need killing.

CHAPTER 16

The waiting room in the surgical unit was packed. Every chair and couch was occupied. Two women across the room from where Craig and Katie sat were conversing in low tones. He heard one woman who was deftly maneuvering two crochet needles tell the other that her husband had been having difficulty urinating for a long time. Whenever he'd go pee, he'd think he was finished, zip up his pants, and urine that remained in the canal would soil his underwear. She said that he always smelled musty—like an old man. Craig watched in amazement as the needles slid in and out of the yarn and hooked around the strain that she held taut with one finger and brought it into the design that was forming.

The TV over the magazine stand in the corner was tuned to one of the local news channels, and Craig tried to get interested in what was being said, but he couldn't stop watching the clock above the door that showed that it was six fifty. They had arrived at the hospital at four thirty, and they began to prepare Martha for surgery at five. Craig had been allowed to stay with her while a couple of nurses and the anesthesiologist fussed around.

Katie sat quietly beside him, reading a book she had so thoughtfully brought along.

"Whatcha reading?" Craig asked.

"It's a police thriller by David Baldacci."

"Who's he?"

"Quite a famous writer," Katie replied. "He's written about ten best sellers."

"What's the name of it?" Craig asked, leaning close so he could see the book's cover that Katie was showing him. *"Hour Game?* Don't think I'd buy a book with a title like that."

"When's the last time you bought a book, Dad?"

"Don't rightly recall," replied Craig as he glanced up at the clock.

They both fell quiet, and Craig looked around the room at the other people that were waiting. A soldier in his camouflage fatigues slouched on one end of a couch near the water cooler that was placed to the right of the restroom door. Beside him was a pretty young woman dressed in a jogging suit that had BYU embroidered across the front.

"How long you think it's gonna take?"

"I'd imagine at least another hour or so," Katie said as she glanced at the clock on the wall. "You want me to go see if I can find some coffee or something?"

"Good idea, doll, but I'll go. Need to walk around. Want something?" Craig asked as he headed for the door. Katie shook her head, indicating she didn't want anything.

While Craig was gone, a strange feeling came over her. Katie had never felt this way before. She felt like she was shaking, but her hands were steady. The shaking seemed to be inside. She was hungry, terribly hungry. She glanced toward the clock; it was all blurry. She couldn't tell what time it was.

"What's goin' on?" It was Craig. One look at Katie, and he knew something wasn't right. Sweat was beaded up on her forehead, and she wasn't focusing. He sat his coffee and a package of six sugared donuts on the end table next to her chair and asked again, "Doll, are you okay?"

"Hungry," Katie replied weakly.

Craig unwrapped the donuts and gave one to her. Powdered sugar dusted her chin and around the sides of her mouth as she slowly chewed and stared at Craig with confused eyes.

Craig noticed a man in green scrubs come into the waiting room and waved his arm, signaling him to come over. The man had gray hair and was a little heavy around the middle. When he stood beside them, Craig spoke up.

"Are you a doctor or something?" he asked.

"I guess I'm or something," came the reply. "I'm an anesthesiologist."

Craig explained what he'd noticed about Katie, and the doctor took out a small penlight and checked Katie's eyes and took her wrist in his hands.

"How do you feel right now," he asked her.

"Little shaky inside," she replied.

"Just relax. I'm going to have a chair brought around and we'll have one of the general practitioners take a look at you."

There was a wheelchair behind the receptionist's desk, and it was brought over to Katie. Once in the chair, she was taken through some double doors and into an exam room. The anesthesiologist helped her onto an exam table and stepped aside as a woman in a white coat with a stethoscope around her neck came up and leaned over her.

"Well, what happened to you?" she asked as she began checking her eyes with a light. She had Katie look in different directions and up and down. The woman then turned to a nurse that was taking notes and taking Katie's vital signs and asked her to get her a glucose meter. In the meantime, the doctor continued to ask Katie questions, and Craig stood by nervously and becoming more and more concerned.

"Has this happened to you before?" the doctor asked.

"No," replied Katie.

"When did you last eat something?"

"I had a donut a moment ago."

"Before that?" the doctor pried. "Did you eat breakfast this morning?"

"I don't think so. Did we, Dad?" She turned her head to look at Craig.

"We didn't have breakfast. Your mom couldn't eat, so I guess we never thought of it," Craig commented.

The nurse returned with the meter and promptly pricked Katie's finger. A bead of blood appeared when she squeezed the finger, and she put some on a test strip.

"It's fifty-two," the nurse told the doctor.

"You're hypoglycemic," the doctor calmly explained.

"What does that mean?" Craig asked, his voice low and filled with concern.

"It means that her blood sugar is way too low. We need to get some food into her." The doctor paused for a moment, then continued. "There's a candy machine in the lobby. Get her a bar. That will kick her sugar up a bit, but we can't leave it at that. She could crash again. While you get her a candy bar, sir, I'll send down to the cafeteria and have some food brought up."

The doctor looked down at Katie and smiled as she spoke, "Is your mom having surgery?"

"Yes, she's having a mastectomy," Katie responded as Craig handed her a Snickers candy bar.

"Your dad doesn't need both of you down. I suggest you contact your family doctor, though, and have some tests run."

The nurse came in with a small tray. There was a plate with scrambled eggs, some hash browns, toast with some jelly in a little plastic container, and a pint container of milk. Katie went after it as if she was starving to death.

"I think you'll be okay," the doctor said. "We'll just roll you back out into the waiting room, and you can take your time eating. If you have any problems, have them come get me. My name is Dr. Shaw."

Back in the waiting room, Craig sat leaning forward, his hands clasped between his knees, watching Katie as she finished off the food they'd brought her. The muscles in his neck were so tight both of his shoulders hurt. The tightness he'd felt in his chest while in the exam room had subsided, but he was still anxious, and he could feel his heartbeat in his temples. It's my fault, he thought to himself. I should have thought to get her something to eat earlier.

"I'm sorry, Katie," he said as he moved to the chair and put his arm around her.

"Wasn't your fault, Dad. I just never thought of it. We both were just thinking about Mom."

They both looked up at the clock on the wall. Martha had been in surgery a little over four hours. Craig stood up and took the empty tray off Katie's lap. While he took the tray to a trash can, Katie pushed the wheelchair over to the receptionist and thanked her for her help.

The time seemed to drag on now. Several times now, doctors dressed in those baggy green scrubs and funny-looking paper booties had come in and spoke with people that were waiting. The young couple that had come with a friend had left long ago. The lady with the crochet needles and the other lady must have gone while they were in the exam room.

The double doors opened, and there was Dr. Mott. She had a paper cap shaped like a bowl on her head, a surgical mask was hanging below her chin, a short-sleeved shirt was buttoned up to her neck, and she had on a pair of baggy green pants held up by a drawstring. She had a pair of those funny-looking booties too.

Dr. Mott walked right over to where Katie and Craig had stood to wait for her. She spoke to Katie.

"I was told that you had some kind of episode. Are you all right?"

"Yes, I'm fine, "Katie responded.

"How's Martha?" Craig wanted to know.

"She did just fine," the Dr. reported. "She's a strong woman, and thanks be to God, there were no surprises."

Katie hugged Dr. Mott and thanked her for taking care of her mom. Craig just sat down, placed his hands over his face, and the two women could hear the sound of his sobs escaping between the fingers. Both women put their arms around him, and Dr. Mott assured him that Martha was going to be just fine and that she was happy to say that they got it all.

"She'll be going to recovery very soon, and it'll be another hour or so before you'll be able to see her. Why don't you both go have an early lunch, and I'll see you in about an hour," Dr. Mott suggested.

Katie took her dad's arm and helped him out of the chair. Craig, with tears still making their way down his face, reached out with his free arm and put it around Dr. Mott.

"I'll always be so grateful to you," he said.

Martha's room was on the third floor of the hospital. The elevator's panel of buttons went from parking 1 and parking 2 to number 9. Craig and Katie were to meet with Dr. Mott in the visitor's lounge on the third floor. Craig pushed the number 3 button and felt the elevator start upward. Katie watched as the floors counted off in the upper right corner. When the elevator reached the third floor, a bell rang, and a recorded voice confirmed the floor, "Floor number 3. Going down," it said.

When the elevator doors opened, they were facing the nurses' station. A sign on the front of the counter read, "VISTING AREA," and an arrow pointing to the left. As they followed the arrow, they passed a men's and woman's restroom, a water fountain, and a coffee nuke. Craig had headed for the coffee nuke, and Katie stopped off at the restroom.

Craig and Katie stood quietly at the foot of Martha's bed while Dr. Mott checked the monitoring equipment.

Craig surveyed the tubes extending from the equipment to Martha's nose and under the bedclothes. He felt a tug in his chest when he saw how pale she looked, how completely vulnerable she looked lying there, with the tubes and needles tapped to the back of her hand where the IV went in.

Now Dr. Mott called out to Martha while she gently patted her cheek.

"Mrs. Spence? Your family is here to see you," she said. "Why don't you say hello?"

There had been a flickering of the eyes, and Martha raised her free hand against the bed rail and beckoned with her fingers. Craig took her hand in his. The usual strength that he generally felt in her hands wasn't there. She barely put any pressure against his. He leaned over to kiss her forehead, and she let a slight smile cross her lips.

"How are you feeling, Mrs. Spence?" Dr. Mott asked. "Can you wake up for me?"

Martha opened her eyes a little and turned her head toward Dr. Mott.

"Had a bad dream," Martha had said in almost a whisper.

"You remember you had a dream," Dr. Mott said. "That's a good thing. What was it about?"

"A big snake was trying to crush me." Martha had begun to make little coughing sounds. She was trying not to cough, each time her face had shown the pain.

"Coughing is good. It helps get rid of the anesthesia," Dr. Mott told her. "What happened to the snake?"

"I think it crushed my chest," Martha said, grimacing as she spoke.

All three, Craig, Katie, and Dr. Mott, were still laughing at Martha's sense of humor when a nurse came in with a plastic container of ice chips.

"These will help with dry mouth" she said. "Now that you're awake, I'm going to take your vitals and see how things are working."

Dr. Mott had assured Craig that Martha was responding nicely and that she would make arrangements for a rollaway cot to be brought in so one of them could spend the night. Martha wanted Katie to stay, and Craig had understood.

Dr. Mott had politely shooed them off while she and a nurse tended to Martha. He had been holding Martha's hand all this time. She gave his a little squeeze and then waved him off. He took one last look back as he'd left the room.

"I'll be back as soon as I see Dad off, Mom," he heard Katie say as she was leaving.

With their arms around each other, they walked to the parking lot. Neither had said a word until they had reached the car.

"She's gonna be all right, huh, Dad?"

"She's gonna do okay," Craig replied. Your mom's a tough old doll."

"When she feels better, I'm gonna tell her what you said about her being old," Katie warned. "Be careful going home, Dad, and don't worry, I'll call you later."

It had been a long stressful day, and as he had accelerated onto the freeway, the tension in his neck and shoulders began to subside. The car was starting to warm up even though he hadn't turned the heater fan on. Just as a precaution, as he began to settle in for the long drive, he opened the front window on the passenger's side a bit and the rear window behind him to keep fresh air flowing. As the time and miles passed, he began to realize that he was going home to an empty house. He was missing her already.

CHAPTER 17

The call had come in to CPI around 2:00 AM. The sheriff's office had an emergency detention at the hospital and needed Fred and Amy to take over. The dispatcher had said that the person being detained was a female, and that she had been picked up on the highway and brought into town by a Greyhound bus.

Fred had gone to the hospital as he usually did when the SO called. Once the gender of the detainee was known, Amy rounded up at least one shift of guards and sent the first guard to meet Fred at hospital lockup. In the emergency room, Fred learned as much as he could about the female being held.

Fortunately, hospital security told him the Greyhound bus had spotted her lying in the middle of I-80 and was able to stop the bus before hitting her. She was in a fetal position, and she stayed that way even when they picked her up and put her in the bus. She wouldn't speak to anyone, just kept humming some type of religious hymn. The bus driver turned her over to the city PD, and they found an envelope in the pocket of the shirt she was wearing that was addressed to Patricia Delgado.

Fred had been led to one of the exam rooms where on a gurney covered with a sheet lay what appeared to be a small person in a fetal position, making low humming sounds.

"Patricia?" Fred said to her in a low nonthreatening voice. "Can you talk to me, Patricia?"

There was no indication that he had been heard. The humming continued, and there wasn't as much as a flicker of movement under the sheet.

Fred started the first report about Patricia. His report included such phrases as: Individual's name assumed to be Patricia; envelope addressed to Patricia Delgado found in shirt pocket; detainee nonresponsive when spoken to; seems to be oblivious to her surroundings; needs to be given a shower and cleaned up when practical; do not allow nurse in room alone with Patricia.

Placing the clipboard on the foot of the gurney, Fred maneuvered the gurney through the exam room door into the long hallway and began the long walk toward the lockup rooms.

The hospital guard walked at the left front edge of the gurney to clear the way and to be of assistance. The transfer from the exam room to the lockup room was always done in this manner unless the individual was violent or potentially violent, then there would be the hospital security person, the police officers that delivered the person to the hospital, and whoever was there from CPI.

On the way, they would pass the nurses' station for the ward where detainees were held. Most of the regular patients on the ward were people recovering from surgery and elderly that had been transferred from nursing homes and long-term care facilities. Several nurses and aides were busying themselves with paperwork, preparing medications, and caring for the needs of patients as the gurney approached. All of them knew that when they saw Fred and hospital security pushing a gurney, things were about to get interesting.

The charge nurse stepped out from behind the long counterlike desk.

"What are you bringing us, guys?" she asked as she took several forms that the hospital security guard had brought from admissions.

"We really don't have a whole lot of information for you," Fred responded. "I'm hoping that it's just a matter of keeping her from hurting herself type of thing, but you never can tell."

"Once you get her situated, we'll get her vitals and see what we can find out," the nurse said.

The door to the lockup room was always kept closed when not in use. It could only be opened from the hallway. The key to open the door was always left in the lock just in case someone locked themselves in.

On several occasions, the doorstop had not griped the tile floor and allowed the door to slowly close while guards or nurses were tending to detainees.

As he pushed the gurney through the inner door of the room, Fred had to decide whether to leave the regular hospital-type bed in the room or take the bed out and just leave the mattress on the floor. There had still been no movement other than that resulting from deep breaths between stanzas of the religious hymns she was humming.

"Don't think we've got much of a problem maker here," Fred said. "We'll just lock the bed down here in the center of the room and play it by ear."

After setting the brakes on the gurney, Fred walked to the large window on the outside wall and, with the blade of his pocketknife, turned a large inset screw that lowered the shade that was inside of two panes of Plexiglas. The two of them, Fred and the hospital guard, left the room, closing only the inner door behind them. Fred stood for a few moments, watching through the glass port in the door. When he was satisfied that Patricia was not an immediate threat to herself, he checked the bathroom to make sure no one had left anything there that Patricia could use to cause damage to herself or one of the nurses.

The light switches were on a wall panel just outside the outer door. This gave security and the nursing staff the ability to control the room's lighting without having to enter the room. It was also one less thing that a detainee could use in some way to injure themselves. Fred stepped out into the corridor.

On the wall across from the lockup rooms was a phone conveniently positioned above a table that was used by the guards on duty. The phone was a direct line to hospital security, or it could be used to call outside by simply flipping a switch. This made it possible for Fred to stay in contact with his people on duty and have direct communications with the sheriff's office. Before the hospital security person had left the area, a handheld type radio had been placed on the table so that contact could be made wherever the hospital security staff might be.

Fred walked through the opened outside door of the room to peer through the port of the inside door. To his surprise, the gurney was empty. The sheets were on the floor and so was the hospital gown that Patricia had been wearing. He could not see the entire room through the port in the door. The right and left corners on the same wall as the door were beyond his view. The windows on the outside wall with the shades closed made a great mirror. Patricia had curled up in the corner of the room to his right.

"How's she doing?" the nurse said as she came up behind Fred.

"Look for yourself," he replied and moved away from the door. As he did so, he noticed Carmen on the nurse's name tag. "Look at the window across the room," he continued.

"Uh-uh, this is gonna be one of those," Carmen said as she moved back from the door.

"I'm afraid so. Now here's the plan," Fred began. "When we go in, you go take her vitals right where she is. I'll take the pad off the gurney and put it down on the floor. That floor is cold, so I suspect that shortly she'll move on to the pad. If she gives any indication that she is going to be violent, you leave the room, and I'll close the door behind you."

Carmen acknowledged with a nod, and Fred opened the door and placed a doorstop so the door wouldn't closed behind them. He could hear Carmen talking to Patricia as he quickly put the pad on the floor against the outside wall so that she could be seen through the door. He hurried back, put the gurney in the hallway, and stood, holding the door just in case Patricia tried to dash for it and where he could keep an eye on Carmen. He didn't want a replay of the Norman Cretin incident.

Norman had disappeared from a drug rehabilitation center in Louisiana. He had been kept strapped to a gurney for three days while he was being evaluated. Tests had detected PCP in his system. Because of his tendency to be aggressive and violent, there were always two security people in the room whenever his arms or legs were released. Generally, this was so he could feed himself or to exercise.

On one occasion, a nurse's aide had come in to take blood pressure reading while his arms were free, and while she was adjusting the pressure cuff, he grabbed both of her breast and wouldn't let go. She cried out in agony as both security officers pried his fingers back to cause him to release her. After that, no medical staff person was allowed in the room when the restraints were off.

After Norman had been detained for seven days, the State of Louisiana made arrangements to transport him back to their jurisdiction.

Steve Lolly had stopped by the hospital to pick up some statements from emergency room staff about the Albert Brown murder case. It gave him an opportunity to check on the situation at the lockup rooms. He had heard from Sherrie about the female that had been found on the highway and decided to check her status.

He could see the female at the guard's table as he had started down the hall. He had visited with her on other occasions. Her name was Joyce and a friend of Sherrie's. When CPI had been looking for part-time people, Sherrie had recommended Joyce, who had been a bailiff at the county court. Her health was such that she could no longer hold down a full-time job. This job with CPI was just what she had needed.

Joyce was of average height for a female—not tall, not short—130 to 140 pounds, with a pretty face framed in a Farah Fawcett hairdo. It was uncomfortably cool in the hallway, so she wore one of CPI's trooper jackets that made her look larger than she really was. Fred had called her to relieve him and take the first shift.

"Hello, Joyce," Steve said as he approached. "How's our little lady doing?"

"Good to see you, Steve," she said as she rose and motioned him to the inner lockup door. Looking in through the glass port, she assured herself that Patricia was decent, and that Steve wouldn't be shocked. Patricia was curled up on the mattress with the sheet over her, but her gown and underpants were on the floor. Joyce stepped back and continued. "This is the way she is most of the time."

"Has the doctor been in to see her?" Steve asked as he peered through the portal.

"Yes, but he wasn't able to get her to say anything. It was different when the priest came by."

"How so?"

"Well, Father Gustoff came by, as he always does when there is a new person in Lockup, and asked if he might introduce himself to the patient. I explained that she probably wouldn't even acknowledge that he was there, but he insisted he'd like to try and talk to her. I went to the door and asked her if she'd like to have the priest talk to her, and she sat right up, didn't say anything, just stared at the door. I told her to cover herself if she wanted to see him. She covered her face with her hands and began to scream, 'No, no, no! He'll rape me! He'll rape me!' So I just closed the door and told Father Gustoff that maybe he should come another time."

"What did Father say?" Steve asked with quizzical smile on his face.

"Father Gustoff is in his early eighties. His face got so red I thought he might have a heart attack. I sat him down in my chair until he got himself together. He blessed himself, blessed me, and went on up the hall."

"She didn't have that reaction when the doctor came by?"

"No, she hardly moved. Just kept humming," Joyce replied.

Steve took out a small notepad from his shirt pocket, made some notes, and again spoke to Joyce.

"What do you make of that?"

"There's a priest out there somewhere that likes girls," was Joyce's answer.

"Was there anything that might give us a clue about where she came from?" Steve was beginning to become really interested.

"The report that Fred left me said there was an envelope found in the pocket of the clothes she had on."

"Where is that envelope now, Joyce?"

"It's probably with any personal belongings she had, and they would be locked up in the hospital security office," Joyce replied.

"I'm going out that way. I'll check on it."

"One other thing, Steve," Joyce said as he was about to leave. "To have gotten where she was found, somebody gave her a ride. I'd bet it was a trucker. If it was, I'll wager he told somebody about this crazy woman he picked up. If it was a trucker and he told somebody, he would tell a waitress at a truck stop. Truck-stop waitresses are like bartenders; truckers tell them everything."

"How do you know that?" Steve asked.

"I used to be one. A truck-stop waitress I mean."

The envelope was pretty dirty, but Steve could tell that it was addressed to Patricia Delgado at an address in Dayton. There was a tear where the state designation would be. It had been postmarked in Sheridan, Wyoming. The date was too smudged to make out. The upper left corner of the envelope, where the sender's name and address, had been cut away. Why? Steve thought to himself. He put the envelope back in the plastic bag and had the hospital security officer lock it away.

It had been near the end of Joyce's shift when she had noticed Patricia looking through the portal of the inside door. Her face was pressed close against the door, and her nose was flat against the glass.

"What is it, Patricia?" Joyce had asked.

"Bathroom," came a weak reply from inside the closed door.

"Okay." Joyce raised her voice a little because she was speaking through the door. "Back away from the door, and I'll let you out to go to the bathroom." Patricia was as naked as the day she was born. She had folded her arms across her breast as if to shield them from sight, but she showed no modesty about how she appeared otherwise.

Seeing that Patricia had backed away from the door, Joyce opened the door. It opened toward her so that it formed a safety barrier between herself and Patricia. The restroom door opened toward her also, forming a pathway for Patricia to enter the restroom. Joyce put a foot against the bottom of each door just in case an attempt was made push past her. There was no glass port in the restroom door and no way to open it from the inside, so once she closed it, Joyce would have to stand by to let Patricia out.

The restroom had only a commode and a sink in it, a small amount of toilet paper, and a few folds of paper towels. Not enough to stop up the toilet. It was the guard's responsibility to replace these items when needed.

"I'm finished," Patricia had called out through the door. "Please let me out."

Joyce opened the door to the room first, then the bathroom door, and Patricia hurried into the room and onto the mattress. Joyce ensured the doorstop was secure and slowly moved toward Patricia.

"Is there anything I can get you, some water or some juice?" When there was no answer, she continued, "Are you hungry?"

"I'm starving," came a weak reply. "Where am I?"

"You're at Memorial Hospital in Rock Springs," Joyce responded. "Why don't you put your clothes on, and I'll work on getting you something to tide you over till lunchtime."

At the nurses' station, Joyce advised Carmen, the charge nurse, that Patricia was communicating and that this might be a good time to collect the information she wasn't able to get earlier. She also requested a sandwich and some juice, and a call was made to the hospital cafeteria. Carmen followed Joyce to the detention room, clipboard in hand, anticipating that while getting required information, she might learn what lead to Patricia ending up in lockup. Joyce peered through the port and smiled. Patricia had put on her underpants, and the gown was draped around her shoulders. Holding the door open, Joyce allowed Carmen to enter the room while she stayed back where she could see what was going on.

Carmen spoke very softly as she approached the mattress, "You seem to be feeling better than you were the last time I was with you," she was saying. "Do you remember?"

"No," Patricia replied.

"I checked your vital signs when they brought you to the room this morning. I wasn't able to finish the process at that time, so if you don't mind, I'd like to do that now. I'll just need to ask a few questions, fill out some forms, and by that time, your food should be here. Okay?"

"Okay," Patricia said as she pulled the gown tighter around her.

"Could you give me your full name?" Carmen began.

"Patricia Anne Delgado."

"Are you called Patricia Anne or just Patricia?"

"I'm called Sister Patricia Anne."

There was a brief pause as Carmen let this revelation sink in a little. She used the time to make some notes on the form clipped to clipboard.

"Are you by chance a nun?" Carmen couldn't help sounding surprised.

"Yes," replied Patricia.

Joyce stared with her mouth open. She wondered if this could be true. A nun in lockup? She was having difficulty with that.

"Well, Sister, could you tell me your date of birth?"

"April 4, 1957."

"What's your address, that is, where do you reside?"

"I live with the Sisters of the Sacred Heart in Dayton."

"Dayton, Ohio?"

"No, Dayton, Wyoming." Sister Patricia Anne replied, somewhat amused.

"What's the address there?" Carmen pressed on.

"I don't remember." There was a faraway look in Patricia Anne's eyes as she tried hard to concentrate on the question.

"Okay," Carmen said as she continued through the questions on the form. "Do you take any medications that we should know about?"

"Yes. Where are my pills?" Sister Patricia Anne looked over at Joyce as she asked.

"What were you taking?"

"I take medicine for cramps, and I take three other pills."

"What are the other pills for?"

"Sometimes I get confused and I take medicine for it."

"When's the last time you took your medicine?" Carmen asked.

"I don't remember ", Sister Patricia Anne replied after a long pause. She had that faraway look in her eyes again.

Carmen continued to make notes while observing Sister Patricia's actions. She was getting up off the mattress, clutching the gown in a futile attempt to keep some degree of modesty.

"What day is this?" She was moving toward the window, and Carmen noticed the bottom of her feet were filthy dirty.

"Today is Sunday," Carmen answered. "Would you pick up your foot and show me the bottom?"

Sister Patricia Anne braced herself against the window ledge and lifted her left foot up behind her. The bottom was bruised, and there was dried blood around what appeared to be several minor punctures.

An aide appeared at the door with a tray. On the tray were a sandwich, a carton of milk, and several cookies. Joyce motioned her into the room, and she placed the tray on the mattress. Carmen took her by the arm and instructed her to get some materials to clean up Patricia's feet and to bring in some patients' socks for her to put on, then she stood beside Patricia and inquired.

"Do you remember where your shoes are? Did you have them when you came in?"

Patricia Anne stared at Carmen with a blank expression on her face. She looked as though she wasn't there but somewhere far off. No one moved, not Patricia, not Carmen, who waited patiently for Patricia to come back, nor Joyce, who was anxious to put the pieces together.

"Where am I?" It was the second time she'd asked. After Carmen told her where she was, Patricia put her hands up to her face and covered both her eyes. The color in her neck and ears began to turn crimson. When she spoke, the sound was muffled through her hands.

"One had to go. I really had to go bad. May the Heavenly Father forgive me." She paused again, and the other two women waited quietly, hardly breathing. "I found some bushes, and I got my shoes wet. I'd never done that before," she continued. "I think I put them in the car, but I'm not sure."

"You have a car?" Joyce blurted out. She couldn't help herself.

"Yes, a little Honda Civic," Patricia replied. "Where is my car?"

"I'm sure it's all right," Carmen said. "Why don't you eat your food, and we'll get you cleaned up, and hopefully, the doctor will come by to see you." Carmen walked swiftly out of the room, and Joyce closed the doors behind her. Joyce went directly to the phone on the wall and called Sherrie at the sheriff's office.

CHAPTER 18

The morning staff meeting had gotten off to a late start because Craig had been on the phone with Sarah Cousins, the county attorney. The case being brought by the ACLU in an effort to force the county to close the jail was on the district court docket for a preliminary hearing next week. Both Sarah and Craig looked forward to it. They had on many occasions tried to interest the county commissioners in discussing a new facility. They were in agreement that though they would defend the county's position, this might be the shove needed to get that discussion started.

Craig had only been in office a couple of years when, during an unusually cold stretch lasting eight straight days, with temperatures hovering at twenty below zero, one of the water pipes in the west wall gave it up. The pipe ran up the wall from the jail's lower floor and coupled to the pipes that serviced the sinks and toilets in the cells. One morning, in the early hours, the elbow that connected the pipes split right at the bend.

The deputy on duty was alerted by yelling coming from the cell block, and when he came out of the control room, the cell block floor was covered with water that came halfway up the side of his shoes. The water was gushing under the door of a utility closet where cleaning equipment was kept, and a freestanding deep sink was attached to the waterline.

It was more than an hour that passed before the public works department could locate and close the shut-off valve. The water found its way into all the cells and seeped through cracks that had been unnoticed. The paneled walls in offices were ruined, and some wire bundles in the communications center that plugged into electrical outlets in the floor shorted out.

Craig had stood firm and refused to allow the county commissioners to bamboozle him into paying for the cleanup, inspections, and repairs out of the sheriff department's budget. This was also the first time that he suggested and formerly requested that consideration be given to replacing the jail facility. The inspections of the building after the cleanup and the stripping away of some of the building's inner façade had revealed some potentially serious structural problems.

Then there was the time when the jail was dangerously overcrowded for months, and the courts were so far behind that prisoners awaiting arraignment or hearings had to be farmed out to the City of Green River and Rock Springs. Craig was certain that the bad conditions would bolster his position and justify a new facility, but all he got was his requests continually tabled at commissioner's meetings if he was able to get on the agenda.

It was during the period of overcrowding that an infestation of body lice occurred. Not only the prisoners were infected. Jail staff was infected too. The entire courthouse complex had to be fumigated, and personnel that worked in the jail along with the prisoners had to be deloused. One of the prisoners was the son of an official at one of the mines west of Green River. The ACLU began their inquiries soon after his release.

After that, Craig spent a lot of time with Sarah. The two of them strategized and met with the commissioners individually, pleading their case. Sarah had recommended that Craig push for an upgrade and expansion of the existing facility. This approach she felt would at least get a conversation started. She didn't expect to dislodge any logjams, but she wanted those commissioners to think about it and justify stonewalling. Sarah had gotten a friend of hers in the county engineer's office to do an assessment and an estimate of cost to remodel and expand. She also enlisted the help of an acquaintance in the zoning and planning department to identify potential sites within the county boundaries on which a facility could be constructed with the least amount of legal wrangling. She wanted to have a plan should she ever end up in litigation and be forced to give the county an out.

Sherrie was first up this morning, and she was really anxious to tell the story about the nun that was in lockup at the hospital. She had two stacks of papers on the table in front of her. They were reports that had been provided by the security people.

"According to what this female is telling the nurses and security, she is a nun, but she doesn't remember how she got to the hospital or where she was going or anything," Sherrie was saying.

Everyone in the room, including Craig, was riveted on Sherrie, including Steve, who was somewhat familiar with the situation.

"I found an envelope in her personal stuff up at the hospital that had been mailed from Sheridan to some place called Dayton," Steve said. "Would that be Ohio?" Steve looked at Sherrie with wonderment in his eyes as he asked.

"Ever heard of Dayton, Wyoming?" After asking the question, Sherrie looked around the room at each of the men at the table. All of them were shaking their heads. "She does remember that she lived with the Sisters of the Sacred Heart in Dayton, Wyoming," Sherrie continued. "I looked it up, and sure enough, there is a Dayton, a very small town west of Sheridan, and there is a small group of Catholic nuns there called the Sisters of the Sacred Heart."

"I've been here all my life and never heard of Dayton," Craig revealed.

"Did she remember how she got down here?" Kevin asked anxiously.

"She says that she has a Honda Civic. She remembers that she had to go really bad and used some bushes. Apparently, she got her shoes wet. Don't know if she got them wet in the snow or if she peed on them," Sherrie said.

"Must be the latter," Craig said. "Hasn't been warm enough for snow to melt. Go on."

"She also says that she takes medication for confusion. Did you see any medication in her personal belongings, Steve?"

"No, just the envelope, no medication, no keys, no nothing."

"Kevin," Craig asked. "You got somebody to put on this?" Before Kevin could answer, Sherrie spoke up.

"Wait a minute," she said, reaching for the top sheet on the other stack of reports. "This is the second time a female has been picked up on the road recently that has been confused and can't remember stuff and is in and out of reality." There was a long pause. Everyone was asking themselves: What's the connection? Craig broke the silence.

"Where's the other female?"

"She's been transported to the state hospital. She couldn't remember anything, and she thought every male was going to rape her. The odd thing is the nun said the same thing when the priest stopped by to see her."

"Was this other female on any type of medication?" Kevin was trying to connect the dots.

"Don't know," Sherrie replied. "She had nothing on her when she was picked up."

"Kevin," Craig said again. "Get somebody on this right away. The lynchpin to this is in that car. Find it, Steve!" Craig continued, "Get a hold of the county that Dayton's in, probably Sheridan County, and work backward. See what you can find out about the sisters and why this nun would be on the road and where she was going."

Craig paused a moment while he made some notes in his pocket notebook, and then he continued.

"What else will be keeping you busy this week," Craig asked of Kevin.

"We had a report of a theft from the Jim Bridger coal mine yesterday. Apparently, someone made off with a bushing." "The hell you say!" Craig exclaimed. "What was it made out of, platinum?"

"Nope, brass," Kevin replied. "The bushing was a replacement for one on the big machines that they use to remove the overburden from the coal seams."

"Who reported it missing?"

"CPI reported it to us. They have the security contract out there. Management reported it to them. No one really knows when it was taken, they know it was there, and now it's gone."

Craig thought about it for a moment and then asked, "What's it worth?"

"About as much as a couple of our patrol cars," Kevin responded.

"Sounds like you'll have plenty to keep you busy this week. How about you, Steve? Anything keeping you up at night?"

"No, boss. Right now I'll have plenty of time to follow up on this nun affair."

"Okay, now just so you'll know, I just got off the phone a while ago with Sarah, our county attorney. The hearing for the ACLU suit against the county and me is coming up this next week. The gist of their complaint is that the jail is inadequate. They say that the physical plant has many problems. Occupancy cells has projecting hardware. There's no recreation area, no access to fresh air or natural light, and the physical layout hinders proper supervision and emergency response, and I, by holding people in the building, am violating their civil rights or something to that effect. Should any of you be contacted by anyone regarding the hearing, refer them to me. I want all of you to be able to do your jobs without having to be concerned about being interviewed by investigators from the ACLU. Just tell them to talk to the sheriff."

Craig looked up at the clock on the wall, checked his watch. He needed to meet Martha at her oncologist's office and had to get going. He slapped his big hands on the table and addressed everybody in the room as he stood up.

"It's going to be a long couple of weeks for all of us, so let's get moving and get a head start."

Doctors and technical personnel from the hospital in Salt Lake held consultations and did follow-ups in Rock Springs twice a week. Patients in Green River and Rock Springs were scheduled by Dr. Mott's office, in Martha's case.

The recovery from the surgery had been no picnic for Martha. The incisions were more painful than she had expected, the itching was almost unbearable at times, and the medication that she had been given really hadn't done much either; it just dulled them a little. Because the mastectomy had been radical, the lymph nodes under her armpits had been removed, and her arms fill with fluid. To force the fluid out of her arms, she had to wear elastic sleeves. Her shoulders were stiff, and they hurt when she tried to do simple things, such as blowing her nose or cleaning her teeth. There was also some loss of feeling.

As he made his way down the hallway to the doctor's office, Craig recalled that it had been two weeks since the surgery and one week since they had removed the drain tubes and allowed Martha to come home. This visit was to check the incisions for any signs of infections and to discuss ongoing treatments that would be followed. He remembered Dr. Mott saying that even though there was a good probability that the surgery had removed all the cancer cells, you could never really be sure, and they had decided to discuss types of treatment during this visit.

The doctor had been very pleased at the way the incisions were healing, and since the sutures were self-dissolving, Martha didn't have to endure them being removed one by one. As for the stiffness and loss of feeling, it was suggested that she exercise, and a technician handed her a sheet with a listing of exercises and instructions. There were shoulder lifts and shoulder rolls, stretches and reaches. Martha's comment to the technician had been that all of the exercises spell H-U-R-T.

After receiving a thorough briefing about carry-on treatment and what side effects could be expected from each, Martha decided to go with a form of chemotherapy that the doctor had called an ACT combination—a menu of three medicines given as treatment, each fighting the formation of any cancer cells in its own way. She would lose her hair; she could expect some nausea after each treatment. Some patients experience mode changes, but every patient reacts differently, Martha was told, so if there were other side effects, they would be dealt with as they manifested themselves. If the incisions continued to heal without any interruptions, the treatments could begin relatively soon. Her next appointment would be in two weeks, and she was told a better assessment could be made then.

After returning home from the follow-up appointment, Martha had an announcement to make. "Okay, you two," she said, "no more soup and soft stuff. I need to reach and stretch and worArms, and I don't want meals in bed anymore. You or Craig can help me to the dinner table."

"Really glad you feel that way, babe. I'm about souped out," Craig said.

The three of them shared a good laugh, and Katie promised a more substantial menu as she walked with her mom through the living room toward her bedroom. Katie walked in front of Martha, who was steadying herself by placing her hands on Katie's waist. It really wasn't necessary that they move that way, but Martha knew that Katie felt better if she felt she was helping, and she enjoyed the attention and the closeness.

As the days passed, Martha got stronger; and moving her arms, pinning her hair back in a bun, or washing up no longer brought tears to her eyes. The itching wasn't as bad either. She was beginning to look ahead to the upcoming treatments, the possible nausea, feeling yucky all the time, the loss of hair, and getting used to having no breasts. Then there was Craig. What he really thought and felt about this new body of hers was beginning to creep into her thoughts. She had noticed him looking at her chest area when he thought she wasn't looking. Even with all the bandaging, she felt that he was imagining how she would look when the dressings were gone. For that matter, he wasn't alone; she too wondered what she'd look like. Maybe she'd get some of those special bras, the ones that looked like they had boobs in them. She could get them in several colors.

Watching Martha deal with the healing process had unleashed some emotions that Craig hadn't been used to feeling. The nights he'd sat holding her hand and feeling her tense up as the pain intensified or the itching became unbearable, and the tears would stream out of the corners of her eyes and down along her ears. His nose would give him away. It would start to run as the tears welled up in his eyes, and she'd open her eyes and squeeze his hand. Nothing would be said, but he'd silently pray to God that he'd give him her pain. He'd wipe the tears from her face with a finger and fight the desire to put his arms around her and hold her; he knew that to move her even a little would cause her more pain. A rush of relief would come over him when she'd finally ask him to give her one of her pain pills.

Now the pain isn't quite as bad, and the itching has subsided some. As he had for the past couple of weeks, Craig sitting in a recliner by the bed, holding her hand, they now talk about the days ahead until one or both drift off, holding hands, comforted in knowing they have each other.

www.ingramcontent.com/pod-product-compliance
Lightning Source LLC
Chambersburg PA
CBHW061544310726
48972CB00008B/2598